OUTLIER ACTION

Book 3 of the Thunderstrike Diaries

WENDY METCALFE

CHAPTER ONE

WHEN PREDATORBOTS WAKE THEY'RE supposed to be instantly alert. Humans tried to bioengineer my lazy lion self into a deadly killing machine. It didn't work.

I yawned, and dragged myself out of my cat bed.

"Morning, Snap. Are you hungry?" Strike asked.

"I am," I said.

"Bahar's in the galley. Go join her, and I'll feed you."

Strike opened the door of my quarters, and I padded down the hallway to the galley. Bahar sat at the table. "Morning, Snap," she said. She trailed her fingers down my neck as I passed her on the way to my breakfast.

I'm a fierce female lion, and I'm not supposed to like people stroking me. I'll let you into a secret: I like Bahar's hugs. She's Strike's captain, and she was currently attacking a huge plate of breakfast stuff, which made my sensitive nose twitch at its many smells. I turned my attention to the haunch of falacca meat Strike's drones had just deposited in my dish.

Strike is the sneaky, smart, sapient machine intelligence of the Human Collective frigate *Thunderstrike*. He's my home. He's a rebel, a righter of wrongs, and was currently part-way through an epic quest.

"Fia just called," he said. "She wishes us good luck on our travels, from her and Rhian."

"We might need it," I replied.

"One step at a time." Strike's voice was calm.

I wanted to snarl at him. This was Nyla and her sisters we were rescuing. They were all in danger, and Strike was so calm, and…

Breathe, Snap. It isn't going to help getting all stressed.

It was how I felt, though. We'd already rescued Fia and Rhian, and taken them to safety on Davion. But we still had to find Zana, Merrill, and my Predatorbot Programme mentor Nyla.

Nyla had outed the secret and illegal project after she got me away from it, putting her and all her sisters in danger. We needed to find them and take them to safety before corrupt President Jorrak could hunt them down.

Strike interrupted my thoughts. "We're under way. Current intel about Pekado Station says it's calm. We might even downjump normally for once."

"That would be nice," Bahar said. "I'm getting tired of

being shot at."

I was nervous as Strike counted down to emergence at Pekado Station. Last time we'd downjumped here an Outlier Action ship named the *Black Vengeance* had tried to board *Thunderstrike*. It hadn't ended well for them. Strike had been forced to kill that ship, something he avoided doing wherever possible.

Yes, you read that right. The Human Collective Starnavy frigate *Thunderstrike* is a conscientious objector.

The Outlier Action people were usually active at the other end of Collective space, in the region the Central Administration called the Outliers. We'd been surprised to see them out here at Ataret Station, half-way to the Central Worlds.

"Place your bets," Strike said. "One, two, or three Outlier ships meet us on downjump?"

"Not funny," Bahar replied. She lounged in the captain's seat, as usual. She wore a set of her everyday faded combat fatigues. Bahar rarely wore her Starnavy uniform. Her skin was the colour of night, and today her fuzzy hair was unbound, and formed a dense cloud around her face.

I settled down in the space beside her seat which Strike had cleared for me. We were in his control room. There were only the two of us on his crew. Plus the twenty troops currently in coldsleep in Strike's cryobay, of course.

"Time to emergence five minutes," he said.

My heartbeat quickened as I waited for the countdown. Through the viewport the roiling slick of greys and reds began to lose its definition. "Five… Four… Three… Two… One… Strike cut off his com the microsecond before transition, as usual. I felt the pressure wave ripple down my flanks as we emerged into normal space. The scene through the viewport altered to black and stars.

"Acquiring coms and nav plot now," Strike said. "And guess what? We're in trouble again."

"What do you mean?" Bahar's voice was sharp.

"I've just been contacted by the *Sirune's Rebellion*. Or rather, her captain. Here's what he has to say:"

A ragged audio file played through the nodes. There was no video. "We claim Pekado Station in the name of Outlier Action. We won't let you abandon our colonies. If you won't listen to us, then we'll force you to listen. You have an hour to surrender control of Pekado Station to our machine intelligence."

"Here we go again," Bahar said.

"Getting data from local Commander. And yeah, we've been drafted into Defence Squad Beta."

"Are we fighting?" Bahar's voice had that nervous tremor that always surfaced whenever the threat of combat loomed.

Strike said nobody really wanted to fight except idiots with stupid ideologies and zero empathy. They were generally the ones giving the orders, who didn't have to do the actual killing. Your average trooper would really rather not be responsible for ending another's life, thank you very much.

But today there'd be no escape from combat. Outlier Action had brought a dozen ships to attack Pekado Station. We were going to get involved. We couldn't avoid it this time.

Beta Squad was ordered to defend the far side of station. Strike fired up his engines and dived below the massive structure, coming up on station's other side, and taking his place at the far right of the defensive formation.

"Targeting *Kyran's Spite*," he said as the thrum of the

wing guns sounded. "Appropriate name for 'em." His voice was light and jokey, but I could hear the tension in it. "Incoming. Evading now."

We lurched violently to port. I hit my shoulder on the navigator's chair, and snarled. The pressure on my body was very uncomfortable by the time he straightened-out. I was used to it, but it was still annoying.

"Firelance away." That was a smart seeker missile, and it twisted and turned to match the *Spite's* increasingly desperate attempts at escape. The ship managed to throw it off twice before the Firelance impacted on its starboard side.

A shower of hull plates fountained out into the blackness, followed by a spectacular flare of flame. When it died down, all that was left was a twisted mass of superstructure.

"One down," Strike said. His voice was emotionless. "One more to go. Targeting *Harrien's Voice*."

The crew of the *Voice* were more adept at dodging attacks, and managed to get in a couple of hits against Strike's shields, but their weapons weren't powerful enough to take them down.

"Bluestreak away," he announced.

Bluestreaks were the nearest thing Strike carried to what

he mockingly called old tech. He could've fired a Hullbuster to smash straight through the ship, but he was limiting the damage he did. It's that conscientious objector thing again.

In the end, the *Redfury* delivered the kill shot to the *Harrien's Voice.*

"Stand down," the Commander ordered. "Resume normal duties."

"Good," Bahar said. "Can we get into port now?"

Strike didn't answer. That was unusual. I opened a private feed line to him and asked, *What's wrong?*

Just got a databurst of ships hurt as collateral damage in that engagement.

And? There was something he wasn't tellimg me.

It's confused. I think a Regulus Lines ship might've been destroyed.

Oh. You don't think it's...

The Dreaming Galaxy's Light? Strike finished for me. *I sure as hell hope not. But I won't know until we get into station. I'm asking Unit contacts there to check for me.* The *Dreaming Galaxy's Light* was the last ship Zana Vatan had been known to serve on.

The Light *doesn't operate all the way out here. It'll be in the Zurrial Triangle.* As an attempt at reassurance, my words were pathetic.

I hope you're right, Strike replied.

CHAPTER TWO

STRIKE'S NEWS MADE FOR a tense journey into dock. Strike still couldn't get a definitive list of civilian ship casualties from that engagement. We just had to hope that Zana wasn't one of them.

We had no idea where the remaining sisters were. Being stupid humans, they'd had a huge row when Nyla outed the Predatorbot Programme, and they stopped talking. We'd already found and reunited Fia and Rhian, but we still had three more sisters to find. The only lead we currently had was to Zana, so we'd decided to focus on finding her next.

Bahar spent the time as we made our way into dock eating, and drinking multiple cups of coffee in the rec area. Her scent was an uncomfortable cocktail of worry and fear. That's the downside of my sensitive nose. I can smell humans' emotions.

"Docking now," Strike finally said. "Ziva says the station's calm." Ziva was a machine intelligence in Pekado Station Security, and she was part of Strike's Special Investigations Unit.

Strike formed the Unit to right the Collective's wrongs.

We expose corrupt Governors and politicians, and we out secret and ethically wrong actions. Like the Predatorbot Programme which created me. We're unofficial, and technically we're traitors.

"Machine intelligences in Station Security here are under observation, so we'll have to be careful with our contact," Strike said. "I suggest you go on station, Bahar, Snap, and see what you can find out about the *Light* from Bansi and Kacela." They were our human members of the Unit here.

"Okay, set up the meeting," Bahar replied. "We're not going to be able to relax until we know the *Light's* okay."

Strike reported to the local Commander over the com. She was one of the most relaxed Commanders we'd dealt with, and didn't demand a face-to-face meeting with Bahar, so we were free to organise our time on station as we wanted.

The Commander had received orders to send ships to the Outliers, on a 'when available' basis. Outlier representatives in the Assembly had been making noise about their colonies being abandoned by the Collective. We knew that was totally our President's unofficial policy, and people were starting to object to it. This 'when available' order was an attempt by President Jorrak to show that he wasn't abandoning the Outliers. Nobody was fooled by it. But it helped us now.

Strike said he was available, and we were ordered to take a cargo load of mixed machinery and coms spares to Lodema Station. That was convenient. Lodema was where we wanted to go anyway. It was the next stop on the Outlier Spine, the line of stations stretching from Central Station to Nerian, at the apex of the Zurrial Triangle.

Bahar and I went on-station just after Second Shift. We were meeting Bansi and Kacela at Greenshimmer Café, in the heart of one of Pekado's redleaf parks, Aldanna.

Strike let us out onto the dock an hour before the start of Third Shift. The berths next to us were occupied by the *Justicefire* and *Hammerlight*, both troop carriers. We came onto the dock as the last of the *Hammerlight's* troops were dispersing along it.

That was the trouble with being a military ship. We always had to berth on military docks, with their better surveillance. I knew that Bahar worried about facial recognition scans. I couldn't think why. She is the legitimate captain of Strike. But you know humans. They fuss and fret over everything. They make life so complicated. And Bahar's scent right now was full of worry.

All I wanted to focus on as we made our way along the dock was avoiding bumping into someone. Humans bruised my nose when they banged into me, and it hurt. This time we made it to the lift lobby without colliding with anyone.

Bahar led me into a lift car. I accessed the station's schematics as it dropped beneath my paws. I was used to lifts by now, and their unsettling movement. We were going down one level, and across to the centre of the station, to reach our rendezvous point.

Humans called these things lifts, but they also went down and across. Strike said many machine intelligences struggled to learn human standard at first, because it had all those imprecise and misleading words.

"No wonder they're always misunderstanding each other," he'd said. "If they just said what they meant they'd get on a lot better."

You might think that Strike didn't like humans from a comment like that, but you'd be wrong. Strike loved some humans, especially Bahar.

Of course, the idea of a sapient machine intelligence

loving someone scared humans witless. So they tried to deny it happened. They gave it the nice, cold, name of 'machine intelligence attachment syndrome'. Stupid humans! They can be so weird sometimes.

The lift stopped at the Aldanna Park lobby, and we walked out through a space decorated with images of red creeping plants. I don't know why humans don't find plants creepy. They have many weird behaviours.

We crossed the busy lobby, with Bahar walking in front of me to shield my nose from blows. The hallway beyond was quieter, and she dropped back to walk beside me.

"We're going in there, Snap," she said, pointing out a nearby arch festooned with a glossy, red leaved plant. "It looks just a jungley as ever. I hope our friends have arrived." Her voice was brittle-bright, trying for carefree petbot owner on leave, but it sounded false to me. I could smell that she was tense. Humans could never hide their true emotions from me.

Bahar feeling anxious was normal just before a meeting with our contacts. We'd recently had a traitor in the Unit who'd tried to out it, and there was always the worry that someone else would do that. Being outed would mean we'd be charged with treason. It would mean death. So I guess Bahar could be excused for her nerves now.

She set off across the dark red grass towards the distant café. I followed her, soon finding that the grass blades were sharp. It was uncomfortable stuff to walk on. I hoped my paws didn't bleed. That would be difficult to explain when I was supposed to be a petbot. Beside me, Bahar's scent had changed to worry, which did nothing for my mood.

I opened a private feed line to Strike and asked, *Why is Bahar so worried?*

She's afraid of what our contacts will say. About Zana.

So she thinks the Light *got destroyed out there?*

I think so.

I cut the connection as we reached the café. Thankfully the grass gave way to smooth paving. I padded onto it, and examined my paws. They weren't bleeding, but I'd ask Bahar to keep to the paved paths on our way out.

Bansi and Kacela were sitting at a table at the quiet end of the café's terrace. I have memories and processors implanted in my chest, and I ran their images through my contacts database. Really there was no need. They were both distinctive; broad women with night-black skin, and cascades of braids falling over their shoulders. I knew who they were. Strike's caution was affecting me too.

"Hi," Bansi said as we approached their table. "Sit down. How's things?"

Bahar settled into a seat at the table. I sat by her feet. "Oh, same as usual," she said, trying to sound casual.

The three humans ordered coffee. Humans drunk buckets of the stuff, then complained that it gave them headaches. They really are a stupid species sometimes.

The serverdrone arrived with their drinks, and after it had left Bansi took a small hand control out of her pocket and placed it on the table. It beeped, and she pressed a button on it.

"Naughty café. Shouldn't be dataminin'," she said.

I opened a private feed line to Strike. *Why didn't you warn us about the bug?* I asked.

I'd already scrambled its inputs. I was trying to do a trackback to the receiving database, but that gadget fried the circuit. I'll send a message out that the café's not to be trusted.

That wasn't any part of a Starnavy frigate's remit, but Strike saw himself as the keeper of the civilian Collective's conscience. Bahar said he needed people to be squeaky-clean. Even after she'd explained that, I still found the idea hard. As far as I could see, no human I'd ever met was honest 100% of the time.

I returned my attention to the conversation at the table. I'd long ago learned to listen to conversations without reacting to them. Humans swung their heads about and waved their hands when they talked, but no petbot did the head-swinging thing unless they were being directly addressed. Anyway, I was a listener this time. I had nothing to contribute here.

"What can you tell me about the attack out there?" Bahar asked. "Why are those Outlier people ramping up their action?" A touch of worry entered her smell.

"We've heard rumours that President Jorrak is pressing the Assembly to declare the Outliers a separate administrative region," Kacela said.

"Which means?" Bahar prompted.

"It's politician-speak for abandoning the Outliers. He wants to cut off all support to them."

Bahar's scent spiked into anger. "Meanwhile, he's still unwilling to address the root cause of overbreeding." Her anger-scent strengthened, and I had to sniff to stop myself from sneezing at it.

"Yeah. Bastard," Bansi replied. "Good 'ol patriarchal misogynist." Now her scent spiked with anger too.

Our contacts were like Bahar. She described herself as a sex-repulsed aromantic asexual, and childfree by choice. It was a designation which had earned her a great deal of hostility from different human males over the years. They seemed to think they had some right to mate with her. Which was weird. Their laws said the complete opposite, and Bahar was quick to tell any hostile male so.

"Do you know which ships got destroyed in that action out there?" she asked. "I'm interested in Regulus Lines ships in particular."

"Only casualties we heard about are Aureus Carrier's *Black Shimmer*, Redshift Tours' *Supernova's Vision*, an' Interstellar Cargo's *Starminer*. Other ships lost sensors, but nothin' important. Got away lucky," Bansi said.

"Sure did," Kacela agreed. Her calm words didn't match her worry-scent.

"'Ain't been bothered by Outlier people here before. Not likin' this change," Bansi snarled.

"Do you know if the Regulus Lines' *Dreaming Galaxy's Light* has been here recently?" Bahar asked.

Bansi shrugged. "Don't keep any records of ship doin's. Too many of 'em. Maybe use your military clout an' talk to Traffic Control?"

I sensed Bahar's scent-spike of annoyance at Bansi's casual answer, and its change to calmness. "Good idea," she said, managing to sound calm. "What other useful stuff can you tell me?"

At the end of station Third Shift Strike secured a private feed line to Ziva. Bahar and I had returned to *Thunderstrike* by then. Bahar was worried about this contact. Kacela had causally mentioned that Station Security was cracking down on unauthorised contacts with its machine intelligences, so Strike had to circumvent their datacrawlers to make the contact.

He used one of his many alias IDs for that, posing as a Starnavy frigate which had been destroyed in the Outliers twenty Standards ago. All his aliases came from ships which had been destroyed, and for which the Starnavy hadn't updated their records.

Humans found record-keeping boring, and often diverted the machine intelligences who should be doing that work onto 'more exciting tasks'. So there were always big inaccuracies in the Starnavy's databases, and we didn't rely on them. But it also came in useful when Strike didn't want to be identified.

We'd waited until Strike was refuelled and his cargo had been loaded before making this contact. If it all went 'pear-shaped', as Bahar called it, we could get the hell out of here smartish. Strike already had an approved departure slot.

Ziva set up the line as audio-only, and seemed reluctant to talk. "I don't have the data you need," he said. "And I need to keep this contact short. Talk to Pranet in Traffic Control. I've been sort of talking to him about… your stuff. I think he'll help. Got to go now." The line went dead.

"That wasn't what I expected," Strike said. "Ziva's always been so helpful before."

"He's really worried about being watched," Bahar replied.

"Agreed. The question is, do we contact Pranet?"

"What do you know about him?" I asked.

"Ahead of you there, partner. Just finished tracking his

ship handling logs for the recent past."

Neither of us asked how Strike got hold of that data. He had a talent for cracking encryption, but he hadn't told anyone else about it. He often got into databases he shouldn't.

"And?" Bahar asked.

"He's made some casual comments that they're not seeing as many Starnavy ships going to the Outliers, and wondering if policy's changed."

"That's a fair observation," I said.

"Yes, but Traffic Control machine intelligences have a code of conduct which requires them to treat all ships equally. Even commenting so casually risks breaking that code. He's already put himself at risk."

"We'd be at even greater risk if he outed the Unit," Bahar said.

"I am thinking of recruiting him," Strike replied. "We need more machine intelligence contacts in good positions here."

Bahar took in a long breath, and let it out again. "Okay. I agree he meets our criteria. Let's hope he wants to join. Do it, Strike."

CHAPTER THREE

STRIKE SET UP A MEETING with Pranet for just after the end of Fourth Shift. That was the start of Traffic Control's quiet period. Most passenger-carrying ships wanted to dock before station's 'night'.

Bahar and I were in the control room for this meeting. Strike wanted our input into Pranet's reactions to his words.

The avatar which appeared on the wallscreen looked a lot like a human's pet dog. It was actually a Kareem, one of the species which lived beyond the boundaries of human space. The avatar's fur was thick, and the colour of golden sand. Its eyes were a startling blue.

"You requested a private meeting," Pranet said.

"We did," Bahar replied. "We've been tasked with studying conflicts involving Outlier Action, specifically cataloguing what civilian collateral damage they're doing in these engagements."

There are times when I don't like Bahar, and this was one. It chilled me when she got all objective, as she called it. That's when she spewed soldier-speak like this from her mouth.

Strike said military language was a careful exercise in distancing humans' emotions from their actions. If you called someone a 'target' you could forget that they had blood pumping through their veins. I got a lot of that attempted programming in the Predatorbot Programme.

There was a pause on the other end of the line. A sidebar appeared on the wallscreen image. Strike was sending us data on the lockdowns Pranet was doing.

He's isolating your line from Security crawlers, he said over the feed to Bahar and me. *A good sign. He doesn't want Security to hear what he says.*

"Sorry about that," Pranet said. "Just had to do certain checks. There's no record of your mission on the official databases."

Bahar's scent spiked to worry. She forced herself to relax. "There won't be," she said. "Central doesn't want to officially admit that the death toll from Outlier Action attacks is becoming substantial. They want us to believe that this is still a minor rebellion."

"You think otherwise?"

"Don't you?" Bahar asked.

There was a longer pause this time. "I have to be careful

what I think," the avatar said. "Thinking could get me in trouble."

"What if I told you there were others willing to think for themselves? Not to overthrow the Collective," she added hastily, "but to force the people within it to fulfil their promises."

The avatar's eyes opened wide. He was interested, I could see that. "What do you mean?"

I saw Bahar take a deep breath. This was the tricky bit. "We know of several individuals who are concerned about corruption and mismanagement within the Collective's structures. They're particularly upset about the Collective President not living up to his election promises with relation to the Outliers. And they're upset that civilians are getting hurt as a result."

"That I can understand," Pranet said. It wasn't quite an endorsement.

What do you think? Bahar sent over our feed line. *Proceed?*

Yes, Strike said. *This is good caution.*

"We've heard rumours that President Jorrak is asking the Assembly to declare the Outliers a separate administrative region. We believe he wants to do that to cut off all aid to the Outlier colonies," Bahar said. "We, and several other ships, have decided we won't let that happen. We're not planning mutiny or rebellion. We're just doing what we can to ensure politicians keep their promises. And when we can, we run supplies to the Outliers."

"Are you asking me to join you?"

"We're still a part of the Starnavy," Bahar replied. "We carry out our legitimate orders. We just do a little more than we're required to to make people's lives better."

"That… is something I think I could sign up to," Pranet said.

"Then you should talk to *Thunderstrike*," Bahar replied. The two machine intelligences could talk using machine code, which no human security system could infiltrate. Strike had wanted Bahar to 'soften him up', as he put it, before he revealed his true identity.

"I'll do that," Pranet replied, and the image on the viewscreen disappeared.

I'll take it from here, Strike said over our feed line.

Bahar decided to go to the rec room to get some coffee and 'stretch out a bit' as she called it while Strike talked to Pranet. In reality, what she did was endlessly pace around the rec area, stopping occasionally to take a sip from her mug of coffee.

After a tense half hour the wallscreen lit, and Pranet's avatar appeared on it. So they were still taking.

"I've been explaining to Pranet what we do in the Unit," Strike said.

The avatar's blue eyes stared right into Bahar's. "You were very cautious before," Pranet said.

"That's because we can't risk exposure. Have you heard about *Firechan*?"

"I know the ship was listed as destroyed on recent update lists."

"She launched a code attack on me," Strike said. "She was trying to out the Unit. It took twenty machine inteligences to kill her." His voice had that flat tone he always used when he talked about killing.

"I see." The avatar's eyes closed. When they opened again it said, "How can I be sure you'll keep your word about not overthrowing the Collective?"

"How can you be sure anyone will keep their word?" Strike asked. "But I have two answers for you. First, neither I nor the other people in the Unit desire to grab power. We're what they used to call a 'check and balance' on the system. We just want to see it operate fairly and properly. Second, the Unit has a Charter, a code of conduct, which you'd be expected to sign up to and observe. File coming over to you now."

The avatar's eyes closed for 2.3 minutes while the machine intelligence controlling it read and considered the file. The avatar opened its eyes again. "This is good," he said. "Very good. Sign me up."

"Great," Bahar replied, and I heard her release the breath she'd been holding. "We're looking for data on the civilian ships which got destroyed in the recent skirmish here, in particular any Regulus Lines ships involved. The briefing we've received from the Starnavy is confused. I wondered if you'd received any Traffic Control notifications of casualties."

"I have access to those. I'll run a search for you," Pranet said.

Bahar flexed her stiff shoulders. I felt just as tense. We

were about to find out whether Zana's ship had been out there in that fight.

CHAPTER FOUR

IT DIDN'T TAKE LONG FOR Pranet to give us the answers we needed. "Just received an updated casualties list," he said. "Three ships were destroyed, from Aureus Lines, Redshift, and IC. No Regulus ships were involved. We don't get many Regulus ships here. Last one was a quarter-Standard ago, the *Galaxy's Veil*."

"That's great news. We're looking for data on their *Dreaming Galaxy's Light*. Do you have any records of it here?"

"I'll check."

The line went quiet for 4.2 minutes, then Pranet said, "I've searched back a Standard. There's no record of the ship here during that time. Is that what you were expecting?"

"Yes. She's probably on the Zurrial Triangle route most of the time. You've been a great help, Pranet," Strike said. "We're leaving now. Remember to run the recognition protocols if you contact anyone else in the Unit. And I don't need to tell you how crucial it is to keep that contacts database safe, do I?"

"I am sapient," Pranet sounded offended. "I know what I

need to do."

"Good. Stay safe." Strike cut the connection. "Well, now we definitely know Zana wasn't here," he said to us. "It's time to move on."

Strike confirmed his provisional departure slot. We had an hour to fill before we left. Bahar fell back on her usual rituals. She went down to the cryobay to check on our troops. She did that twice a day when we were shipboard and things were normal.

Her checks were totally unnecessary. Strike ran the cryo systems, and he could've told her the readouts were fine. But, being human, Bahar had to check those readouts with her own eyes. Sometimes Strike still got annoyed or upset by her doing that, but most of the time he accepted it was just a weird thing she did.

She came back to the control room half an hour before undock. "So far, everything's still calm," Strike told her.

"Then let's get out of here before that changes." Bahar dropped into her seat.

Strike handled the undock and turnaround as efficiently as

always, and soon we were on our way to the jump point. The line out was busy, and that always put Strike on high alert.

We'd had instances of ships scanning us before. We think they'd been searching for Predatorbots. And Chan had used another Predatorbot to force me to attack Strike. After that attack he'd taken out my behaviour module. We no longer had to worry about people endangering us that way.

We got nearly to the jump point before Strike said, "Alert. The *Lanceflow* is scanning me. It's a small Starnavy courier."

"The sort of ship the Starnavy uses for special ops," Bahar replied.

"Indeed. I'm sending back a normal pattern and not recognizing that I'm being scanned. They're not moving in close, so I think it might just be a general security sweep."

"But why scan Starnavy ships?" Bahar asked. "Has something changed here?"

"There's nothing on the most recent updates."

"I wonder if our President is up to something," she suggested.

"We'll try and find out when we get to Lodema. We've got some useful contacts there. And... scans have stopped.

Nobody's hailing me. Looks like we're going to make it out okay."

We were scheduled to jump in twenty-two shipboard hours, so Bahar and I went to sleep before then.

I slept in the First Officer's quarters, in a large cat bed which Strike had had made specially for me. He'd washed my blankets, and his drones had straightened them out for me. They smelled of grass from Earth, and some new flower scents from Reeva which I'd said I liked when we were down there. That was one way Strike showed his love for people.

I settled onto my side and curled up my legs. As I closed my eyes Strike said, "Sweet dreams, Snap."

Don't believe that sapient warship machine intelligences are heartless. The affection Strike put into his voice then would rival the most loving human.

I woke ten hours later, feeling totally rested, for once. I'd slept off all my tension about recruiting Pranet into the Unit.

Strike fed me in my quarters, and after I finished my meal I went to the control room, leaving Strike's drones to clean up my mess, and to grumble about it, as usual.

"Bahar's doing her usual round of the cryobay," he said as I sat down in the cleared space beside the captain's seat which was mine. This morning, exasperation showed in his voice.

"No, she's not," she said from behind me. "I'm back. So what's on our schedule for today?"

"Jump, hopefully," Strike replied.

"I sense a but there."

"The 'but' is that jump point scans have identified a small object close to the jump point which Station Security can't identify. Our departure time's been pushed back while they investigate it."

"Knew it couldn't be that easy," Bahar grumbled as she dropped into her seat.

"They've sent a minesweeper out. They think it might be a hostile device."

"Surely someone's not trying to destabilize the jump point?" Bahar's scent spiked with fear, and made me sneeze.

"Starnavy's been known to do that in the past."

"Yes, but we're not at war with anyone now," Bahar replied.

"Or are we?" Strike asked. "Receiving a databurst from

Starnavy local Commander now."

CHAPTER FIVE

IT WAS A TENSE HOUR until the minesweeper came on-station. The ship turned out to be *Firesweep*, and Sweep was part of the Unit. Strike sent out a sitrep request, which Sweep would answer when she'd got the time.

Her answer came at the same time as Traffic Control resumed normal service towards the jump point. "It was a lashed-together device from Standards-old components," she said. "We're lucky it didn't randomly go off."

"Any idea who put it there?"

"Pekado Station Security are trawling the jump point records now. Ziva's sent what she knows, which isn't much. At this stage, we don't know. You're safe to go through, though."

"Thanks. I'll leave you to the forensics," Strike replied.

He cut the line and boosted his speed. "Let's get out of here before those idiots do something else stupid."

We came up to jump two shipboard hours later, surprisingly fast, given our slowdown earlier. Traffic Control had obviously given ships in line permission to exceed the usual speed limits, in an attempt to clear the backlog. No station wanted ships backing up. The complaints and lawsuits rolled in pretty fast then.

"Coming up to jump in half an hour," Strike announced as Bahar finished yet another cup of coffee in the galley. "They let us spread our wings." He sounded satisfied.

I often wondered if Strike felt bored being constrained by Starnavy orders. Our lives were so regulated by orders and rules, but I guess we needed them to stay safe out here. Most of the time Strike didn't complain about them.

"Jump in five… four… three… two… one. As usual, Strike cut off his com at the last microsecond before insertion. I saw the corners of Bahar's mouth quirk up in a knowing smile. Strike complained about her rituals, but he had just as many of his own.

The weirdness of transition swallowed us up, then the scene through the viewport changed to the usual mixture of shifting greys and dull reds. I used to shiver at the sight of that unreal reality when I first came aboard Strike, but I long ago got used to it.

Strike says we're here on the universe's permission, and as long as we keep to established procedures we'll be safe. He says the consciousness of the universe is glad to have other minds moving through it. I guess that counts as Strike's religion, but he'd deny it if you said that. Sapient machine intelligences can be just as complicated as humans.

"Lodema Station, here we come," he said. "Hope there aren't any nasty surprises on downjump there."

The stations serving planets along the Outlier Spine were evenly-spaced. The jumps between them were all classed as Moderate. For Strike, this was easy stuff, and he almost didn't have to concentrate as he made his way through the well-travelled hyperspace route.

The Starnavy said it posted human crews to command sapient machine intelligences, to ensure they followed orders. The reality was very different. Strike ran this ship. If Bahar gave him an order he disagreed with there was no way she could force him to carry it out.

The truth was that sapient machine intelligences needed company. Just like humans, they didn't fare well in solitary confinement. That was the real reason Starnavy ships were always crewed.

Our downjump at Lodema Station was normal, and we

made it into dock without anyone trying to attack or scan us. The Starnavy databurst which Strike had received just before we went into jump was going to be useful here. Starnavy ships had been tasked with meeting local civilian shipline managers, to discuss travel security with them.

"President Jorrak revealed his plan for the outliers at a confidential Supply Committee meeting of the Assembly yesterday," Strike said. "Not surprisingly, it's leaked out, and it's causing a great deal of unrest in the Central Worlds."

"It's reached here pretty fast too," Bahar observed. "And no doubt it'll embolden Outlier Action to make more attacks on us when they receive the news."

"That's the worry. Our role is to tell civilian managers about Outlier Action, and encourage them to review their security procedures."

"So how does this help our search for Zana?" I asked.

"Quite a bit, actually. Nobody's started civilian liaison duties yet, so I made sure we got the meeting we needed. Regulus have just opened a shiny new regional office here, so I think you should pay them a visit."

"Why do they want an office here?" Bahar asked.

"It's pretty much the mid-point of the Outlier Spine route,

so where better to build up an expansion of your business back towards the Central Worlds?"

Oh, right. Did that mean Regulus were about to abandon the Outlier routes? I hoped not. They were what Bahar called 'a major player' out here.

"We're docking in ten hours' time," Strike said. "You two go get some sleep. I'll start tapping our station contacts for data."

I took Strike's advice, and went to sleep. I woke hungry, as usual. When I first came aboard, Strike had wondered how I could be hungry when all I'd done was sleep. But that's the nature of lions. When we're not chasing down our dinner we spend most of our time sleeping. Tourists love to watch us big fierce pussycats sleeping as innocently as a newborn fluffy kitten.

Can you hear my sarcasm there? Tourists turn us into something safe, when in reality I could easily rip a human's head off. That's what they wanted to bioengineer me to do, after all. Stupid humans.

I finished my meal and left Strike's clean-up drone to sort out the mess I'd left. If Strike wanted tidiness he could always print me just the juicy meat and not the stringy bits, but no, he had to print 'authentic' meat. I dealt with it as an 'authentic' lion should: by leaving the stringy bits uneaten.

You know that thing about rituals? This was another one. A ritual which said everything's fine, there's nothing to worry about.

Bahar said Strike and I acted like a bickering married couple sometimes. She said some humans snarked at each other like that all the time. Why would you do that? I thought you married somebody because you loved them. Humans have no end to their weirdness.

We docked 22.3 minutes later. It was just before station's First Shift. Bahar and I were both in the control room as Strike locked onto the dock. Bahar ran her eyes down the long list scrolling across the wallscreen. It was stuff about dock connections, and she didn't need to know it, but she said she got 'vibes about how the station was doing' from watching how they handled our docking.

Vibes are another of those weird things humans claim guide their actions. If a machine intelligence confessed to doing something on a hunch it would be classified as glitching. Humans glitched all the time, but they only got investigated when what they became dangerous or hostile.

"Had some luck," Strike said as Bahar eased out of her seat. "The *Black Velvet's* just docked."

"Ebony's here?" Bahar asked.

"Yes. We should be able to get a reliable update on what our President's up to."

"Useful."

"She suggests a catch-up on station. So you two are going ashore to meet her avatar – before you talk to Regulus."

Strike could've had an avatar of his own to send on station, but he'd never done that. He said that too many machine intelligences lived through their avatars, forgetting who they really were. He'd never had any desire to be 'a substitute human', as he put it, and didn't want that interface.

Strike described himself as a 'pure' machine intelligence, one who interacted with the universe only through his shipboard processors and memories. Bahar had argued with him about that, calling him disingenuous. She'd pointed out that he controlled lots of different drones to give him data. Strike had said that was different. Drones were just other peripherals, new sets of sensors, tools to be used for data-gathering.

Bahar hadn't been convinced by his answer, and the argument flared up again occasionally.

Bahar and I went on station after the whirlwind of First Shift shift change had ended. We were heading for the Deep Circle Café, right in the centre of station's Level Three. They advertised the place as 'the safest café on station' to nervous travellers.

The bonus was that Ebony's avatar was joining our contacts, so we should get to know what our, increasingly unpopular, President was up to.

The station was busier than usual at this time, and many of the people we passed scurrying about in the hallways smelled worried.

"Is that a station thing, or something wider?" Bahar asked when I told her about the scents.

Strike opened a feed line to us. *It's partly because Station Security did a recent crackdown on 'carriage of illegal and dangerous goods'. The trouble is, they got it wrong, and hauled in a lot of innocent carriers for questioning. All those companies have now launched legal actions for damages against the station. And a couple of regular cargo lines have rescheduled their routes via Revecca.*

That's quite a detour. And expense, Bahar said. *They must be really upset with station.*

They are. But Security are still hauling people in for questioning. That's why I said you should dress military.

Oh, right. Bahar had kicked up against that. Strike could've just told her why then, but he hadn't. I think sometimes he enjoyed puncturing her calm.

Bahar tugged her tunic down, and stepped into the lift lobby. It was busy, and we had to wait 6.2 minutes to get a car, even with the help of the Unit's machine intelligences in station Logistics. There seemed to be no evidence of a boycott of the station today.

The lift car let us out at another very busy lobby, and Bahar had to push her way through the crowd to get to the exit. I stayed behind her and kept my head down, hoping nobody bumped into my nose.

We came out onto the leisure deck. The café was 10.6 minutes' walk along the footway. It was an austere place, with dark grey metal panelled walls. It was arranged in three circles, with the lower one being the biggest circle.

Bahar opened a feed line to Ebony. *Where are you?* she

asked.

By the North Red entrance. It's quieter over here.

On our way over, Bahar said.

As we walked around the café's curve I saw people dressed in a selection of uniforms, some military, and some in civilian shipline colours. It was a perfect place for the exchange of data between them. Strike had chosen the venue perfectly, as always.

There's Ebony, I said.

You couldn't miss the ship's avatar. It was tall and solid. It stood at a table by the wall, scanning the room for us. It was dressed in a formal tunic and trousers of wine-red silk, with one modest line of gold braid trimming the tunic's collar and cuffs. She looked like a wealthy shipline owner, not somebody to mess with, despite her night-black skin and long locs.

Bahar waved to her, and steered me between the cluster of tables to the waiting group. Our other two contacts were Axelle, a human with the palest skin and hair I'd ever seen, and Kojo, her opposite. His skin wasn't quite as dark as Ebony's, having more brown than black in it, and his hair was a wavy halo of brown.

The two humans were already half-way through mugs of coffee, and Bahar wasted no time in ordering hers. "So what's the news, Ebony?" she asked as she sipped her coffee.

"A Central contact's just sent me a file of President Jorrak's appearance before the Supply Committee yesterday. The file was classified, so somebody took a risk sending it to us. It confirms that he's asking for permission to designate the Outliers as a 'special administrative region'."

"Is that why the Outlier Action people are stirring?" Bahar asked.

Ebony nodded. "Yeah. Think they've already got word 'o this. We're gonna see a whole load 'o trouble if he continues with this."

CHAPTER SIX

"JANIYA LINES HAVE PULLED out of servicing the Zurriel Triangle route recently," Axelle said. "Their ships are big enough to leave, but the smaller carriers are stuck in the Outliers. We've heard rumours of difficulties in obtaining vital parts for ship repairs. A couple of cargo haulers are currently stuck in the 'yard at Dracen Station, awaiting new parts."

"That's not good," Bahar replied.

"You asked about Regulus," Kojo said. "They're still out there, but shipline's gettin' noisy about problems they're havin'. Think they might'a got somebody new at the top recently."

"Interesting," Bahar said. "Do you think that might signal a change of policy?"

"Not sure. Regulus made its wealth servicing the Outliers. Won't abandon 'em easily," Ebony replied.

"They will if the colonies fail," Axelle said.

The news our contacts had about the Outliers was disturbing. Outlier Action had seized control of the colonies on Dalfon and Ilani, killing the elected Governors and taking over. Judiciary were on their way out to deal with the murderers. That was unsettling news, and we could only hope that they didn't repeat the action elsewhere.

Nobody knew who was leading Outlier Action, and we'd been tasked with passing on any data we received on them to Central. So far, their actions had been occasional and didn't seem to be centrally organised.

"What we really need information on is the *Dreaming Galaxy's Light*," Bahar said. "We have an interest in tracking down a crew member there."

"You doin' Judiciary's job now?" Kojo asked sharply.

"What?" Bahar was confused by the comment. "Oh, no. We want to ensure her safety. She's not in trouble."

"Good. 'Cos we heard a 'Navy ship arrested some officials on Kumarr."

"I haven't heard about that," Bahar replied. "I'll ask Strike to investigate when we get back."

Axelle glanced down at me. "We think we saw a Predatorbot on Olianna Station. It looked a lot like you, Snap."

"Do you have a file of it? Can you send it to me?" I asked.

Axelle looked surprised for a moment, then said, "Sure. I forgot you had processors."

That was part of what the Predatorbot Programme did to me. I have processors and memories implanted in my chest. I'm some kind of weird half-machine intelligence.

The images appeared in my mind, and I saved the file to my memories. I watched the cat walk along a hallway somewhere. It was another of my kind, I was sure of it.

"Snap, are you okay?" Bahar trailed her fingers down my neck, and I realised I'd frozen up.

"I'm sure that is another Predatorbot," I said.

"Right. We should look out for it on our next visit there, then."

The conversation moved on to other things, and I let it go. I was focused on the Predatorbot. I was certain it was the cat we'd nicknamed Shadow. How would he react if he came across me on Olianna? Who was the person he was with in those images? Strike wasn't the only one who needed to do some investigation.

We returned to *Thunderstrike* an hour after Fourth Shift start. Regulus Lines had been resistant to a liaison meeting with us. It was only when station released an announcement about the danger Outlier Action posed that their local manager had agreed to see Bahar.

Bahar's meeting was scheduled for an hour before First Shift the next station day. I don't know if the manager thought he was going to inconvenience her by insisting on meeting so early, but that wasn't going to work.

Bahar put on a captain's semi-dress uniform for the meeting. It had several rows of gold braid, and her captain's and service badges were prominently displayed. She also wore the hated hat, perched on top of her thick braids.

She tightened the chin strap and said, "Are you sending a drone with me?"

"Nope. Already into their office security systems. Useless, as usual," Strike said.

"Behave yourself."

"I'm only observing. I'm not doing anything."

"Except stripping their confidential data," I said.

"That's of no interest to me. I'm not going to give it to anyone."

This is why Strike describes what we do as 'morally grey'. In theory, he shouldn't have access to that data, but often knowing stuff he shouldn't helps him to keep stupid humans safe.

The Regulus offices were two Levels down from Strike's berth, and on the other side of station from him. Bahar got to them ten minutes before her interview time. The Regional Manager kept her waiting beyond then, of course.

Bahar settled into a soft seat in the window, with her back to the aide behind the reception desk. She sighed dramatically. "I do wish these silly men would stop their stupid power plays. Don't these people realise they can lose their trading licences if they piss people off enough?" She spoke as if she was talking to someone, and loud enough for the aide to hear.

There are listening devices here, Strike said over our feed.

I was counting on that. There was an edge of anger to her tone.

2.3 minutes later the manager's assistant summoned her to his office. "Mr Varenquoc will see you now."

"Thank you." Bahar was all grace, rising slowly to her feet, and showing none of the irritation I knew she felt.

The office the aide showed her into was huge. One whole side was a mirrorwall, looking out onto the business plaza outside the office. Another wall had floor-to-ceiling plas windows, overlooking a large open-plan office beyond.

I see he has a large corner office, Strike sent over the feed.

What? I asked.

That used to be a thing managers aspired to, Strike explained. *A large corner office with windows on two sides.*

I told you humans were weird. Why did it matter how many windows their offices had? I just don't get them sometimes.

I think he wants to spy on his employees, Bahar replied.

The Regulus Regional Manager sat behind a huge fakewood desk which I was certain had a shield. That was interesting. Did people attack him regularly?

Bahar stood in front of it, and held out her hand to shake. He had to stand up to take it, and I sensed his reluctance. Eventually he did, and clasped her hand in the briefest of handshakes.

Does he have a disability? Bahar asked over the feed. *I feel guilty for forcing him to stand up now.*

Nothing I can find, Strike replied. *But he does have a reputation for being churlish.*

And my skin colour doesn't help, Bahar said.

She hadn't been invited to sit down, but she did anyway, keeping her back straight in the chair. "I'm sorry to disturb your busy day," she said, "but the Starnavy has been tasked with warning the civilian operators here about the mounting Outlier Action threat.

"I don't know if you're aware that renegades claiming allegiance to that group murdered the Governors of the Ilani and Dalfan colonies. There is increasing unrest in the Outliers, and we are asking all Outlier operators to review their security arrangements."

"Our security arrangements are robust. Our new CEO's seeing to that," he growled. "We're a civilian carrier. We don't let the Starnavy order us around."

Rude, Strike said over our feed.

"It isn't a case of ordering anyone around," Bahar replied. "It's a case of passing on information which will make your organisation safer."

"We don't need your help," he snapped.

Bahar stood up. "In that case, I won't detain you any longer." Before he could reconsider she let herself out of the office, strode past the confused aide, and out of the complex.

That didn't go well, Strike observed as she strode along the footway.

Bahar's back was straight. She shrugged her shoulders in an angry gesture. *He's a lost cause. We'll get no help from him.* Despair bled over the feed line from her.

So we get our information elsewhere, Strike said soothingly. *Get back to my shipbody. We'll think what to do next.*

Bahar appeared at our berth 12.2 minutes later, and Strike opened the lockout gate and let her in. She seemed angry as she came into the control room, but her scent told a different story. She was worried. She plopped into her seat and said, "That wasn't good."

"The guy has a reputation for being unhelpful," Strike said. "The data I've found on him tags him as a ruthless climber. He must've thought he had it made managing this new regional office. And then you came along and rained on his parade."

"I didn't…"

"He'd see it that way. Let the stupid fool take the consequences of his actions." Strike had long ago run out of patience for humans who didn't take essential advice.

"It's the consequences for Zana I'm worried about," she

said.

"You… Oh, we've just acquired a new worry. The local Commander's throwing his weight around. He wants to send a 'protective force' to Revecca Station, to defend against Outlier Action attacks."

"We really don't want to be sent there. It's out of our way," Bahar replied.

"No. And we certainly don't want to be held there for months. And… he's just got permission for the draft."

Neither of us asked how Strike had got that data. Someone in the Unit had passed it on.

"I can't get a departure time for half a day. Traffic Control's locking down military slots I think, though they're not confirming that."

"So what do we do?" I asked.

"We've suddenly developed a nonlethal sublight engine fault which will keep us in port until it's checked out. Kojo's just logged the fault. We're officially 'for repair' status as of now."

Our contact Kojo was the Team Leader of Fault Assessment, Repair Group Three, at Lodema. He was a really handy contact to have. He'd handle the fake fault investigation.

"Strike fixes it again," I said.

"Well, I did," he replied, refusing to rise to my tease. "Let's see if we can find out what's really happening at Revecca, shall we?"

CHAPTER SEVEN

THE REPORTS STRIKE RECEIVED from Revecca Station confirmed that Outlier Action were causing trouble there, but this time they hadn't attacked ships. They'd sent a bunch of heavily-armed thugs onto the station, in an attempt to take it over. 103 of them had been killed in the action, and 11 innocent bystanders.

"I confess this bothers me," Strike said. "A lot of people came ashore there."

"They won't be leaving, though," Bahar pointed out.

"And their ships have been impounded," Strike added. "Revecca's 'yard is busy stripping out their drive units as fast as they can."

"That's as morally grey as we are," Bahar said.

"Not really. All the ships were stolen from someone else."

"Oh, right. So when does our task force leave?"

"At Second and Third Shifts tomorrow. All military departure slots for that time period have been grabbed by the task force."

"Just as well we're stuck in port, then," Bahar observed.

"Yes. And... Kojo will be bringing a team to assess our

fault at the start of Third Shift."

"How convenient."

"Isn't it?" Strike agreed.

I thought they were going to start an argument then, but Bahar yawned instead.

"Go get some sleep, you two," Strike said. "We've got a long day tomorrow."

Another thing humans don't want to think about is the idea of machine intelligences watching them sleep. They put sapient models into their infrastructure, then complained when those intelligences did their jobs.

I think Strike secretly enjoyed watching over us at rest. Not because he could learn all our intimate secrets, but more because it brought him closer to us. I think he saw himself as a benevolent father keeping his children safe.

He'd scoff at me if I said that, and call it a ridiculous notion, but he wouldn't outright deny it.

Anyway, I slept well, and Strike fed me as soon as I woke. That was another way he showed his love for me. He was constantly tinkering with his printer recipes, improving the 'nutritional quality' of the meat he fed me.

After he'd done his usual scold about me being a messy cat he let me out of my quarters. "Bahar's in the rec area," he said. "Pounding the treadmill."

That meant she was stressed about something. "Has anything happened overnight?" I asked as I padded down the hallway to join her.

"There's been another raid on Revecca. The raiders took over a cargo handling hub and killed the supervisor. It's over now."

"Oh. Right." Strike would be feeling guilty about refusing to go with the task force there.

"Bahar's angry about it."

"There's nothing we can do about that now."

"I told her that. It only made her more angry with me."

"You couldn't know that would happen."

"I think she thinks I should've known." Strike made an exasperated noise. "That because I'm a sapient machine intelligence I shouldn't make mistakes."

"It wasn't a mistake."

"I wasn't there to help defend those people."

"Has the task force arrived there yet?"

"No. They're still in jump." Strike's tone was puzzled.

Then he said, "Oh. It wouldn't have made any difference, would it? Thanks, Snap." Strike opened the rec room door for me.

Bahar had stopped punishing her body on the treadmill, and was busy glugging down a container of water. Sweat formed a bright sheen over her dark skin.

I don't understand humans and their exercise thing. They make themselves breathless and sweaty, then claim it's good for them. That doesn't sound too attractive to this lazy lion. Strike was supposed to be finding a treadmill for me. I'm kind of glad he hasn't found one yet. I'm not sure whether I'd use it.

Bahar turned to me as I arrived. "Morning, Snap. Another day of doing nothing."

"A day of doing research," Strike replied. "Ebony's not due to leave until Fourth Shift. There's a backlog in civilian slots out, thanks to the Commander. Station's threatening to sue the Starnavy for indemnity against their financial losses."

Bahar sighed. "I do wish humans would lose their obsession with money."

"Got to look good for the shareholders," Strike said. The

scorn in his voice was obvious.

"So we need to do something positive with our time in port. What research should we do?" Bahar asked.

Bahar and I went on-station just after the start of Second Shift. We had a brunch date with Ebony and Axelle.

The station was quiet, but there was an underlying feeling of tension in the hallways. Civilians seemed jumpy, checking all around them as they walked instead of engaging in their usual mindless conversations. It never ceased to surprise me how many conversations humans could have which meant absolutely nothing.

Maybe it's because we Predatorbots had to be taught to speak that we only say things when we have something useful to say. I struggled to learn human standard for 6.7 months.

We met our contacts in The Cosmic Vegetable this time, a place which prided itself on offering the weirdest-looking vegetables from around the galaxy. I don't get that either.

I'd already eaten before we left *Thunderstrike*, but I certainly wouldn't be tempted by the large plate of purple, gold, orange, and red stringy things which Bahar was served.

It looked like eating multi-coloured grass to me. Only prey does that.

"I've got an update on Regulus," Ebony said. The avatar lounged in its seat, totally comfortable in this world of humans. "It's in a databurst I received from Central 2.5 hours ago. The Interstellar Licensing Authority has marked Regulus's files as 'of concern'."

"Not good," Bahar replied.

"Indeed. They only do that when there have been a series of incidents involving a shipline. So I started digging around to find out why. Their safety record was always 'Satisfactory' until a Standard ago, but I've found some records of recent failures."

Bahar sat up straight, and Ebony raised a soothing hand. "They're only minor things. Nothing life-threatening. Like failure to replace a blown short-range coms receiver on one of the backup arrays. It's all stuff like that, failing to repair backups."

"Backups are there for a very good reason," Bahar replied. "Are they penny-pinching?"

That was another saying I'd had to get her to explain. She showed me a penny in a museum once.

It's possible," Axelle said. "We've received a rumour that the colony on Katarz may be being abandoned."

"Katarz is a key part of the reason the Zurrial Triangle route exists. It might be a serious threat to the viability of the route if the colony does go belly-up," Bahar said.

"Indeed," Ebony replied. "So far it's only a rumour, but it fits with Regulus putting a shiny new office here."

"So where do we look for the *Dreaming Galaxy's Light*?"

"Ship's never put in here, according to our Traffic Control friends. The majority of Regulus's ships are still working the Outliers. I'd say your best bet is still to go there."

Bahar and I returned to *Thunderstrike* an hour after Kojo's team had found the fake fault in Strike's engines and fixed it. The task force going to Revecca had departed by then, and Traffic Control had returned routing to normal.

"I've got a provisional departure slot for an hour," Strike said. "Which... I've just confirmed, now that you're back on board."

"Are we still heading for Olianna?" Bahar asked.

"Yes, we are. In the absence of any better information, I'm sticking with my plan to go to Ralziel Station. Let's hope we pick up Zana's trail then."

CHAPTER EIGHT

OUR LINE OUT WAS a slow one, and Bahar and I went to sleep while we made our way to the jump point.

I try not to sleep through jump insertion. It turns my dreams very weird. Once I dreamed I'd grown two huge wings, and my face had extended into a long beak. I could fly, too. It only lasted 3.1 minutes, and I woke with a start, thinking I'd jumped off a tall mountain crag. The dream had triggered my processors to record it, so unlike humans who don't remember theirs, I had a permanent record of it.

When I showed it to Bahar she said I'd become a dragon. I said I'd never seen one of those, and she told me it was a mythical creature humans had invented.

That's something else I don't get about humans. Their planets are full of the most magical creatures, yet they never appreciate them. They've spent centuries killing them off, just to get more of those credits they can't take with them when they die. They're weird creatures.

I woke this time 3.1 hours before jump, and Strike fed me before I went to the control room. Bahar wasn't there when

I settled on my belly in my cleared space.

"I'm glad you're here early," Strike said.

That meant he was fretting about something. "Why?" I asked.

"Kojo found a genuine fault in my systems. Not in the engine control suite, but in the anchoring point for the casing. He said it had started to work loose."

"So why is that a problem?"

Strike paused for a moment, then said, "I'm fretting again, aren't I?"

"You are. So why couldn't you find the fault?"

"That's what worries me. Kojo said that, technically, it wasn't a fault yet."

"So why is it worrying you?"

"Because the idea of stuff working loose and me not being able to spot it is terrifying."

"Then you're just like the rest of us," I said. "Humans don't know they have things like cancer until something happens to prompt them to get a scan."

"That's... how can they bear being in meatbag bodies with all that stuff going on?"

I snorted. "They don't have a choice. Just like me."

"And a lovely meatbag body you have, Snap," Bahar said from behind me. She plopped into her seat and ran her fingers down my neck. "So, are you okay, Strike?" There was a hint of challenge in her voice.

"Yes… Yes I think I am now," Strike said. His voice sounded firmer. "Prepare for jump."

I tried not to notice Strike's extra diagnostics runs as we made our way through hyperspace. The not-quite-fault had scared him, and he was doing what he could to reassure himself about it.

He sometimes mocked humans and their fear of space. Maybe this not-fault would give him a bit more understanding of fragile humans. And a touch of humility. I could hope, but I wasn't counting on it.

Strike spent the time he wasn't fretting about his drive analysing the new data he'd got about Outlier Action. The Starnavy files he'd received at Lodema contained some attempts at tactical analysis of the organisation's actions and aims.

He ran as many scenarios as he could think of, and an hour before our downjump at Olianna Station he finally ran out of ideas. "It's no good," he said. "I've searched every tactical playbook I can find, and their actions don't fit with any recognized campaign. I'm beginning to think they really are a bunch of disgruntled amateurs."

"Disgruntled amateurs with weapons still kill people," Bahar pointed out.

"Yes, but the point I was making is that I can't anticipate their next move. Their attacks look random."

"Maybe they are if nobody's in command. One redneck gets all riled up, then gets killed. Another one takes his place."

"You're assuming the leaders are male," I pointed out.

"Women aren't as stupid as that. We plan better," Bahar said.

Strike snorted. "I know a lot of misogynists who'd violently disagree with that."

"While proving how unreliable their testosterone makes them as leaders."

"We've done all this before," I said, stepping in to stop the argument escalating.

"Anyway, we're due to downjump soon," Strike said. "Let's plan some scenarios in case things are hot then."

For once, downjump was normal. We were on a longish line in, and wouldn't dock for another five shipboard days.

That gave Strike lots of time to talk to Ishara and our other contacts on station. Ishara was a machine intelligence in Olianna Station Security, and also part of the Unit. She was one of our most useful contacts here. Strike also put out a lot of requests for data on Regulus Lines, enlisting the help of people in civilian organisations who had good links to the Central Worlds.

As we came into dock Ishara contacted him. "Station's quiet," she said. "And we haven't had any trouble for a couple of months. You're safe to come ashore."

"Then we will," Bahar said.

"You should try the new pancake place we have here. Everybody I know who's been there loves it."

"You on commission from them?" Strike asked.

"Nope. Just passing on the comments I've received from friends."

"Okay. We'll take your recommendation, Ishara. When should we meet you there?"

I had a whole roiling mass of feelings running through my mind as I walked down *Thunderstrike's* ramp beside Bahar. I wore my armour, but it was retracted, and looked like a petbot's fancy metallic coat. I set the camouflage programme to show a cute lion cub's head and a fake petbot manufacturer's garish logo. Strike said it looked so hideous that people would take one look at me, screw up their faces in disgust, and move on. That was just the reaction I wanted.

We still haven't discovered how many of my kind are still alive, but we do know that Central Security have issued an order to find us all. I don't know what they plan to do with us when they find us, but I'm betting it wouldn't be good. I'd rather stay undiscovered, thank you.

The dock was quiet. The two berths next to *Thunderstrike's* were empty, and the two beyond them were occupied by small fleet support hauliers. Ishara said all the warships had been drafted into a boundary defence force, and there was a constant patrol around the station.

Strike didn't want to be ordered to endlessly circle Olianna for months, so he'd put in a request to the shipyard for a maintenance check on his engine 'repair'. He knew that status would get passed on to the local Commander, and would make us unavailable for immediate draft anywhere.

I concentrated on being a good petbot as I walked along beside Bahar. The news that another Predatorbot had been seen here unsettled me. I hoped I didn't run into it. I thought I could fool it, and it couldn't access my behaviour module because I didn't have it any more, but I still felt anxious.

Bahar took me to the pancake place, which was two decks down, but on the same side of station as Strike's berth. Our contacts were already at the café. Ishara's avatar presented as a tall, white-skinned woman with long, thick wavy red hair. It was dressed in a bright jade robe, and the avatar wore strings of red, yellow, and green beads around its neck. Ishara's alter-ego was as far from the meticulous Station Security machine intelligence as she could get.

Our other contact was Harrikan, a short, elderly, white-skinned man who was almost bald. He wore scarlet polish on his long nails, and his jacket was a patchwork of eye-chasing designs and colours. He was a recent recruit to the Unit, added for his research skills.

Our contacts certainly didn't blend into the background, and Bahar's deep blue silk tunic and trousers looked dull beside their brightness.

After the usual greetings and food ordering, they settled in to talk. Harrikan proved his worth immediately. "I've been researching Regulus Lines," he said as Bahar cut into a ridiculously tall stack of pancakes laden with fruit and sticky syrup. She'd be on the treadmill tomorrow, working off the extra weight all that sugar had given her. Humans have a really complicated relationship with food.

"And?" she asked.

"The old CEO, Naor Tamaz, died a year ago. The official records, and all the company's announcements, say that 'he took his own life after getting into personal debt'."

"Personal?" Bahar queried.

"This is where it gets interesting." Harrikan leaned forward, steepling his painted fingers together. "That's what they're saying officially, but... There's been a lot of re-financing of the shipline's debt in the last Standard. The new CEO is his brother, Boaz Tamaz. Boaz has quite a reputation, and it's not a good one. Some people I've spoken to suspect there was a difference of opinion between the brothers. Some rumours even suggest Boaz murdered his brother."

Wow, that wasn't good.

"There's worse, I'm afraid. "We've heard that Boaz is sexually harassing his female crew members. If they say no to him, he's demoting them, and falsifying their records to wreck their careers. There are a dozen lawsuits filed against him for that already. He's also more reckless than his brother. He's ordering ships back into space after the minimum of repairs and maintenance."

That would explain the Interstellar Licensing Authority's 'of concern' note on the shipline's file. This was getting seriously worrying.

"The worst rumour is that Boaz has started reassigning female crew members to his flagship the *Regulus Glory*. That one's a luxury liner, and the rumour is that the man is building a harem of women there."

"What?" Bahar almost exploded out of her seat. "That's…"

"Yes, it is," Harrikan replied. "It is just a rumour right now, and I can't find anyone who will definitely confirm it, but it is worrying."

"It sure is," Bahar replied.

Up to now, we hadn't been worrying about how long it took us to find Zana. But this information had given a new urgency to our quest. We had to find her before this sleazy CEO could harm her. And we still didn't know where she was.

CHAPTER NINE

STRIKE HAD BEEN MONITORING our conversation, of course, and as Bahar said goodbye to Ishara and Herrikan he opened a private feed line to Bahar and me. *I want you to go meet a new contact now*, he said. *Her name's Ismat Mohallawe.*

So why are we interested in talking to her? I asked.

Because she's a ship captain. And she's recently resigned from her captaincy of the Silver Prosperity. *That's a Regulus Lines ship.*

Oh, right, Bahar said.

And I've received an advisory from Ishara that a strike force may be on its way in here.

Do we think Outlier Action are trying their luck here now? I asked.

It's possible.

Should we come back to you?

It's more important for you to follow up this new contact. She isn't Unit, so be careful.

Right. Give me the location details, Bahar replied.

Strike sent the data over on the feed. *Howin and Rance*

are in wake-up, he told us. *They'll be awake in an hour. I'll send them on station as soon as they're moving.*

Let's hope we don't need them, Bahar replied. *Okay, we're on our way to the new contact.*

We had to go up two levels and in towards the centre of station to meet our contact. We were going to a café in Nakkos Park. The park was mis-named, because it was actually a forest. It had massive trees, which had been rescued from their native planets and brought here for safety.

That might've been a bad move if Outlier Action wrecked the station. No, that wasn't going to happen. The Starnavy would see them off.

When I first came aboard *Thunderstrike* we'd had long discussions about why humans needed armed forces. Could we imagine a universe where the Starnavy wasn't needed? I know Strike wanted to believe in that ideal, but even he had to admit that sometimes you had to stand up and fight for your rights.

The park was gloomy and oppressive, the light levels low. There were lots of places to hide behind the thick tree trunks to take a shot at someone. Why had I thought of that? Strike waking up Howin and Rance had unnerved me. He only did that when he seriously suspected trouble would erupt.

After 7.2 minutes' walk along a winding path the space opened-out into a sizeable clearing with the café in its middle.

That's Ismet, Strike said over our feed line.

She was sitting alone at a table at the edge of the café space. Her skin was not quite as dark as Bahar's, and her hair was arranged in braids pulled tight to her head. She wore a black tunic and trousers which looked like it should be a uniform, but it bore no badges. She waited quietly for us to approach her.

"You must be Ismet," Bahar said as we reached her table.

"I am. I assume you're Bahar?"

"That's me, and this is Snap," she said, running her fingers over the top of my head.

"Join me. I heard you were looking for information on Regulus Lines."

"I am. I have a female friend aboard one of their ships, and I've heard some rumours I don't like about the line. I'm really hoping you can't confirm them."

The serverdrone arrived, and Bahar ordered her favourite coffee. She got really excited about the different beans and the ways they were roasted. I didn't get that either.

Ismat sighed. "Don't get your hopes up. I've just resigned my captaincy of the *Silver Prosperity*. It took me a decade to work up to that position, and now it's gone." The angry edge to her voice was clear. It obviously hadn't been an amicable split.

"We're investigating rumours of wrongdoing at the shipline. It's not an official investigation, but if you tell us something that proves their illegality we'll go to the authorities with it. You ought to be warned about that up front."

"Thanks for being so honest. It all started to go wrong a Standard ago, when Boaz Tamoz became CEO of Regulus. His brother Naor was CEO before that. I'd met Naor several times over the decade I worked for them. I liked that guy, and he cared about the people who worked for him.

"Then he died. They're saying he committed suicide over money worries. I don't believe that. Naor was a careful, thoughtful kind of guy. I can't see him being reckless enough to lose his money."

"So what do you think happened to him?" Bahar asked.

"The handover was sudden. We had no advance warning.

I woke up one morning to an all-fleet message that Naor had died overnight and that Boaz was now CEO. I don't know what to think about his death."

"May I ask why you resigned your captaincy?" Bahar said.

Ismat stiffened-up, as if trying to defend herself from attack. "I left to avoid being raped. The rumours about Boaz sexually harassing women were already circulating. About a month after he became CEO he came aboard the *Silver Prosperity* when we were docked at Nerian. Half of my crew had already gone ashore when he came to my cabin and demanded sex.

"I told him to get out, and he threatened to ruin my career if I didn't say yes. The moment he left the ship I collected my things, went ashore, and resigned. It hurt. I'd worked hard to get that position, and it was all gone in one man's sleazy approach.

"I've been surviving on contract assignments ever since. My skills are good, and proven. Boaz's smear campaign of me failed. And now that the rumours about him are getting out life should become easier for me."

Bahar took a long breath, the kind of breath she took to

steady herself when she was furiously angry. "You shouldn't have had to suffer that."

"No, I shouldn't. You said you were looking for information on a friend?"

"Yes. Zana Vatan. She's First Officer on the *Dreaming Galaxy's Light*."

"I've never met her, but I'm pretty certain the ship's still on the Zurrial Triangle route. Boaz doesn't spend much time there. I don't think he makes enough from his private side hustles in the Triangle."

"Oh? Is he dealing in something illegal?"

"I got told not to ask."

"Right. So it probably is, then."

"If you're looking for your friend I'd say head to Ralziel if your ship can make that jump, and ask around there."

"Oh, we can make that jump," Bahar replied. "You've been a great help, Ismat. I hope you find a good permanent position soon."

We started on our way back to *Thunderstrike* half an hour later. This time the station was busy, and there was a feeling of nervousness to the people scurrying along the hallways.

As we stepped into a lift car Bahar secured a feed line with Strike and asked, *Has something happened here?*

Not yet. But the Black Sister *has just docked. They're not actually raiders, but the crew cause trouble most places they go. Station's just put out an order to watch them. And you watch yourselves. They're known pickpockets.*

That shouldn't bother us, Bahar said. *We're not carrying anything valuable.*

Even so, be careful. Howin and Rance are awake. I'm sending them on-station now to see what they can discover.

The lift car doors opened onto a lobby crammed full of people. I dropped back behind Bahar, to avoid getting my nose bruised. She fought her way over to the dock, which was almost as busy.

The last thing I remembered before I blacked out was a man shoving a stunner into my neck.

I woke to find I was strapped onto a gravsled. I had a blanket over my body, and I was tied down at each ankle.

I forced my rising tide of panic down and tried to think. Someone had snatched me. Where was Bahar?

Beacon on, you idiot, I thought, and switched on the

secure transmitter. If those people were looking for the signal from a Predatorbot's behaviour module they'd be out of luck. I no longer had mine.

My beacon was part of the new coms suite of processors which Strike's med unit had implanted into my chest when he took out my behaviour module. Which meant the secure frequencies it operated on were unknown to anyone at the Programme.

Receiving. Strike's voice came through faintly to me. That meant he was using a shielded feed line. *Bahar got stunned too. Howin and Rance are on their way.*

He broke the contact, leaving me alone in my world of fear and confusion. I couldn't rely on Bahar to rescue me. Think, Snap! The best thing you can do now is collect data for evidence.

I set my processors to record my captor's conversation. I kept my eyes closed. I didn't want them to know I was awake.

"D'yer think this is one of 'em?" That voice was a man's, rough-edged by too much drink or drugs, I suspected.

"Who knows? We're getting paid for turning it in. That's all I care about." That voice was female, and silky-smooth.

I could imagine her cheating men out of their money in bars.

"Gotta go down two Levels to reach the ship." The man was whining.

I tried not to react to his words, but they frightened me. If they took me off station it would be much harder for Strike to rescue me.

What if the ship they were taking me to had a med suite, and they put me into it? They'd find out I have no behaviour module. Would they leave me alone then? No. I had a huge amount of memory space implanted, far more than any petbot. They'd start trying to break into my memories and…

As my captors guided the gravsled into a lift car my panic took hold full force.

CHAPTER TEN

THE LIFT LET US OUT onto a civilian section of dock. "Damned system," the woman growled. "We're four berths from the ship."

"Gotta avoid discovery," the male replied. "That's our instructions, right? An' who's payin' us? Don't like this deal. Smells of the Collective."

I forced myself to relax and keep my eyes closed. This was sounding more and more like a Predatorbot Programme operation.

"Yer think this thing's important? What if it's just a fancy petbot? Gonna draw attention to ourselves for no reason then. Can't afford to do that." He was whining now. I was glad he wasn't on Strike's crew. I couldn't have stood that constant complaining.

"Not sure." For the first time the woman sounded doubtful. "Just turn it in, then we'll see."

Howin and Rance are on the dock, Strike said. *They want to see which ship you're headed for before they rescue you.*

That made sense, but it could be a tricky intercept if things went wrong. I tried to relax, and forced myself to keep my eyes closed. If they thought I was still out they couldn't order me to do anything.

"Just told the *Golddigger* we're on our way in," the man said.

Sending our troops to that berth, Strike said over our feed line. *We'll intercept at the gate.*

I didn't reply, but I wanted to say 'Get this right. It's my life you're dealing with'.

The gravsled slowed down and the man said, "Open the gate, Huss."

"Halt!"

I couldn't avoid jumping at that voice. It was Rance at his roaring best. "Station goods check. Please provide your paperwork for that petbot."

"Who the hell're you?" the woman snarled. I risked opening my eyes. My captors were both in front of me.

"Station Security. We're investigating piracy reports. The *Golddigger* doesn't exactly have a perfect reputation, does it?" Rance's voice was full of scorn.

So Strike had been digging around in the records. Or, more likely, Ishara had been stripping the Station Security files.

"Get out of my way." The woman snarled. "I will shoot

you."

"Not if I shoot you first." Howin's voice was measured and cold. "Now, are you going to show us that paperwork?"

Two bright energy bursts were answered by two more. I couldn't see who'd shot who from my position. Then someone grabbed the gravsled's tether and pulled it. I was on the move again.

I opened my eyes and saw we were going away from the raiders' ship. That had to be good, didn't it? A feed line opened and Howin said, *Lie still, Snap. We've got you. I'm impounding these goods for further investigation.*

Get me untied!

I will as soon as we're off this dock. We'd draw too much attention here. Lie still. Howin's voice had the tone of command.

Then be quick. I didn't like her commanding me. I didn't like being tied up and unable to move. Unable to run away.

Humans did this to their own kind. They called their own people slaves, and they put rings around their ankles and chained them up. Or worse still, put collars on them and chained them up by their necks. One of the most advanced species in the universe treated its own kind as if they were pieces of plas.

Most of the time I like most humans, but this slavery thing turns me cold. That's what Fia Vatan had been, someone captured and forced to work in that mine. I hope the sisters are still safe on Davion.

We're going into a security check station now, Howin said over the feed. *We'll have you off that thing in a minute.*

A door clicked shut behind us, and she came around to my head. "I'll do a quick forensics scan of the bindings first," she said, and took a scanner out of her jacket pocket. Now I was getting impatient, and I raised my head to watch her work. She must've got the message, because she finished the scan quickly, pulled on a pair of gloves, and undid the bindings.

She dropped them into an evidence bag and sealed it. "Ishara might be able to do something with the fingerprints and DNA traces on those. Let's get you on your paws." She flipped the gravsled over on its side, and I snarled as my paws touched the deck and took my weight. "What's wrong, Snap?" she asked. Her voice was gentle now.

"My leg hurts." I swung my head down to indicate I meant my left front foot.

"Sit down and I'll check it."

She took a portable med kit out of another pocket, and I sat down on my haunches. She lifted my left front leg and gently turned it around, and a memory from the Programme triggered.

It was the day Nyla had said sorry to me. Nyla is an animal neuroscientist, and she'd been hired to check our development. But they hadn't told her what the Programme had done to us.

When she found out she'd gone ballistic and demanded the removal of our behaviour modules. Then she came to the pen we cubs were in and apologized to us. Most of the cubs were angry with her, but even then I understood it wasn't her fault.

She'd lifted my front leg and held onto it, like Howin was doing now. She'd looked me in the eyes, and said she was sorry.

"You've got a small cut on your leg." Howin jerked me out of the memory. "I'll clean and close it."

The spray stung, but I was used to that too. I'd learned not to bite medics healing me back in the Programme.

"Let's do a skinheal pass on this," Howin said, and ran the

wand over my leg. "How does that feel?" She released me.

"Better," I said. "I can walk now."

"Good. 'Cos we're getting out of here."

She led me through the station, along a maze of narrow hallways that were maintenance tunnels and security accesses. Ishara must've given her the route. It was a boring journey along endless grey halls, but eventually Howin ushered me into a lift car.

As soon as the doors closed Ishara contacted us. "I'm routing you priority to *Thunderstrike's* dock," she said. "Traffic Control have found a cluster of incoming ships they're worried about. No action has been taken about them yet, but you don't want to be in dock when a muster order's issued."

"We sure don't," Howin replied. "Thanks, Ishara."

"All part of the service."

The car let us out on *Thunderstrike's* dock. It was busy with troops in uniform hurrying along. Strike contacted us as we came onto the dock.

Hurry aboard, he said over the feed. *All these troops have been recalled to their ships. I'm sure the local Commander is about to issue some orders. We want to be gone before he does.*

We're on the dock, Howin replied. She upped her pace, using her legendary presence to force a way through the crowd for us, and soon we were back at *Thunderstrike's* berth. Strike opened the lockout gate for us and I trotted up the ramp behind Howin. As soon as Rance was aboard the outer airlock door closed.

"Undock initiated," he said as we came through into the hallway.

So he was really worried. He hadn't done the airtightness checks on the airlock we'd just left before he undocked. That wasn't cautious Strike.

"We have a fast line out, thanks to Ishara and her friends. She 'lost' us off the 'available' lists," Strike said.

"Handy," Howin replied as we made our way up to Deck Two in the lift. "Any data on those kidnappers?"

"Go to the rec area. There are some interesting complications you should know about."

That didn't sound good, and Howin didn't ask any more. The lift let us out on Deck Two, and Howin set a fast pace along the hallway towards the rec area. Bahar was there, and she sprang up as I approached, kneeling down beside me and throwing her arms around my neck. "I'm sorry, Snap. I lost you," she said. "I was trying to protect you from the crowd. Then six men pushed in behind me. I thought they were just rude, but… they had to be part of that gang. They separated us. By the time I had enough clear space to turn around they'd snatched you." Her apology was breathless, and her hug was too tight. "I'm so glad you're unharmed."

She released me, and I met Howin's questioning gaze. I saw surprise in her eyes, and maybe a little jealousy too. Howin was what humans called a lesbian, but she had no current partner. I guess that would be difficult if you spent most of your life in cryosleep. Now I wondered if she'd been attracted to Bahar.

"So what's the news?" she asked.

Strike lit the big wallscreen. "These thugs are wanted in five systems for theft and illegal trading." A dozen mugshots came up on the screen. All of them were male and white-skinned, and had a rough look to them. "They put in at Revecca before they came here. Two of them were arrested there for assaults on station."

Strike went quiet for 2.1 minutes, then said, "The local Commander's just ordered all available troops to muster here. Fortunately, we're not available. I'm using one of my alias IDs to get out of here, so we won't be as fast as usual. Now, onto more interesting stuff. My inquiries about the *Light* are beginning to bring in results."

He sent an image of a ship to the wallscreen. It was a big cargo haulier, one of the biggest hulls operating. "That's the *Dreaming Galaxy's Light*, and from the analysis of the images I've done the ship looks sound. This file was captured a quarter-Standard ago, as the *Light* was coming into Nerian Station."

"So it looks like she is still travelling the Zurrial Triangle route," Bahar said.

"Indeed. I still think the best place to look for Zana is there."

"So we're bound for Dracen?" Howin asked.

"We are."

"You keeping us awake?" Rance asked.

"I am, for now. Ishara's not sure of the situation at Dracen. There was trouble there a month ago. We might need you."

CHAPTER ELEVEN

OUR LINE OUT TO THE jump point was long. Bahar smelled tense, although she was doing her best to look relaxed.

Howin and Rance spent their time analysing the files Ishara had sent Strike. She'd sent him records for the last Standard, from both Station Security and Traffic Control. Howin and Rance were looking for patterns which might indicate Outlier Action's game plan.

Strike said humans sometimes found stuff by 'gut feel' that he didn't see. I got the impression he was annoyed that humans' imprecise senses could sometimes produce a better result than his perfect machine intelligence analyses.

I was on high alert all the way out to jump. I was expecting Strike's deception to be discovered at any moment, and for *Thunderstrike* to be hauled into some task force.

It didn't happen, and we got to the jump point without challenge. "Going to give ourselves away as we jump," Strike said. "Our alias doesn't have engines this powerful."

"It is what it is," Bahar replied. "You can't always cover everything."

"True. Jump insertion in three… two… one…"

The transition was as clean as always, and Bahar relaxed as soon as we were though it. "So, we've run away again," she said. "Somebody's going to spot the pattern eventually."

"You're forgetting we have a large Unit," Strike replied. "Our machine intelligence allies change records where necessary. We don't have a trackable trail."

"A century ago that would've got you all killed," Bahar said.

"What do you mean?" I asked.

"Humans created the first AIs, then scared themselves witless about thinking machines. They got all panicked about the bad things the machines would do."

"And why was that?" Strike's voice was scathing. "If we were prejudiced, it was because your algorithms taught us to be."

"So how did we get to machine intelligences working alongside humans?" I asked.

Strike snorted. "Necessity. Humans wanted to conquer the stars. But they didn't have the skills to do it. They needed machine intelligences' computational abilities. So they compromised by insisting that every high-level and sapient machine intelligence got an ethics and morals database installed."

"Which you still have," I said.

"We do, but not in the form humans originally gave it to us. They taught us never to challenge elected officials."

"You do that often."

"Yes. It's nuanced. We don't challenge elected officials who do what they should, but we will oppose crooks and rogues who misuse their positions. And deciding that makes use of a lot of code we wrote for ourselves."

"I can think of a few officials who'd have a fit if they knew that," Bahar said.

"Then they're welcome to try living without machine intelligences."

"We couldn't."

"Exactly."

Bahar stretched, and looked at the roiling greys and reds passing by outside the viewport. "Well, I'm trusting you to keep us safe through this weirdness again. And I'm hungry. Feed me, Strike."

While we made our way to Dracen Station Strike worked

through a data dump of files Ishara had sent him.

He was looking for patterns of trouble which could indicate that unrest in the Outliers was growing. The trouble which Dracen had suffered a month ago was a fight between two wealthy merchant families. One had based their operations on Ilani, the planet right at the outer edge of the Zurrial Triangle route. The other was based on Huali, close to Ralziel Station.

The trouble had taken the form of what Bahar called a 'turf war'. One merchant accused the other of operating in his exclusive territories. The other responded by saying there were no exclusive territories – unless you were a gang boss, of course.

That allegation of illegality had incensed the merchant, and the insults had started flying both ways fast. Then it got dangerous. They'd started trying to block each others' ships from getting into dock at stations. Both of them had recently been issued with reprimands – and massive fines – by the Interstellar Transportation Authority.

Then some of their captains had started refusing to carry out the dangerous orders. Several had resigned, walking off their ships and leaving them stuck in dock until new captains were appointed. So not only was Dracen dealing with crazy navigation choices by some captains, it was also having its traffic management options reduced by ships blocking its docking slots.

"Might need to do some fancy moves on downjump if the craziness is continuing," Strike said.

"Which is another reason why we need machine intelligences. To save us from our own stupidity," Bahar replied.

"Now you're getting dangerously close to suggesting we control you."

Bahar laughed. "I reckon you'll always find idiots you couldn't control."

"Maybe. We're about an hour from emergence," Strike replied. "I suggest you two go eat while things are still calm. Howin and Rance have already finished demolishing large plates of stuff. I'm going to need more printer stocks if we keep them awake much longer."

I was in the control room with Bahar for our downjump at Dracen Station, and both of us felt tense. Strike emerged, and immediately went shields-up. He delayed turning his beacon on until he'd stripped the current traffic advisories from the nearest buoy.

He also received an update from Ursal, a human member of the Unit who worked in shipyard scheduling. Ursal said things were currently calm, so Strike turned on his beacon the second Traffic Control made the request.

In theory, it was always supposed to be turned on, but the Starnavy often ordered ships to turn them off for covert exercises. Strike was a Starnavy frigate, and nobody ever scolded him for running without it.

"The local Commander's briefing has come in," he said. "No current trouble. None anticipated. So we can get into dock in a straight line this time."

Bahar looked at the nav plot Strike had put up on the wallscreen. "Is it my imagination, or does that line-in look a little thin?"

"It's certainly quieter than I'd expect for a major Outlier Spine station – at least, coming from the direction of Central space."

"So perhaps traffic to the Outliers is slacking off."

"Or perhaps it's just a quiet time of station's day. You can find out when you go ashore."

"To do what?" Bahar asked.

"Meet Ursal. Who just happens to have found a recently-resigned captain from Regulus Lines."

"Oh."

"Yes. And she's willing to talk to us. I said we were following up reports of illegal operation in the shipline."

"Right. A new lead is always good. Any problems here?"

"Nope. We're going to have a nice, boring ride in for once."

Thunderstrike docked 1.5 hours after the start of station's Second Shift. The dock we were on was military as usual, but it was unnaturally quiet. Bahar and I went ashore first. Howin and Rance would leave separately, and do some snooping around of their own. They'd keep an eye on us, though. Secretly, I was glad they wouldn't be far away if things went 'pear-shaped', as Bahar put it.

I'd been scared by my kidnap on Olianna Station. I'm sure those thugs had been paid to pick up Predatorbots. Hopefully Strike would get an update from Ishara on that. And hopefully there wouldn't be another set of thugs waiting for us here.

That's the trouble with travelling spine routes. Everybody can guess where you're going next.

"I hope this café we're going to has a good menu, Snap." Bahar's voice had false brightness in it. She was dressed in a faded scarlet silk pants and tunic set, and was wearing another of the heirloom necklaces she'd inherited from her mother.

"My mother really did have hideous taste," she muttered as she settled the chunky piece with its red stones more comfortably around her neck. The setting looked like silver, and the central stone, which was supposed to be the body of a dragon, was some cheap red glass.

"If anyone wants to rob me of this they're welcome. They'll get a nasty surprise when they come to melt down the silver. This thing is junk."

She complained about her mother a lot, but I knew that humans often did that when they really missed the person they were complaining about. Humans are a mixed-up species.

We went down two levels, and through a leisure hub, until we came to a café called Green. It really was green, with a riot of shiny large-leaved plants growing up the entrance pillars and trailing down from the roof.

Bahar led me inside and the green continued, with plants growing up the walls of the entrance. Trailing plants of green, red, and purple twined through them, and dangled down. Here and there a scarlet flower peeked out. The light level in the access was low, and for some reason, the place made me feel uneasy.

We brushed past the plants until we came to a large circular area which was raised up out of the gloom. Our contact sat at a table at the far end of the circle.

I had to thread my body between the tables. As I passed one a human child of around twelve years old reached down and stroked my head. "Cool petbot! Just like a real fierce lion," the boy said.

I forced myself to relax. Bahar turned and glared at the kid, who got the message and removed his sweaty hand from my head. Bahar locked gazes with the kid's mother, who quickly looked away.

She moved on swiftly. I was relieved that what Bahar called 'a scene' had been prevented. She was not above telling human females to tell their sticky, noisy, brats to behave themselves.

That never went down well with the parents, and often ended in a shouting match, with Bahar telling the 'selfish breeders' as she called them exactly what she thought of their decision to breed multiple children.

This time we got to our contact without conflict, and as Bahar sat down I settled at her side. "Sorry about that, Snap," she said. "Is your head sticky?"

"Not this time."

"Good." She turned her attention to our contact. "Hi, Ursal. Long time, no see." Ursal grinned. He was a short, stocky, white-skinned man who wore his white-blonde hair long in a thick plait. "How's things?"

The serverdrone arrived, and Bahar ordered her coffee and a substantial brunch. When the drone had gone Ursal said, "It's quieter than usual here. We're getting less traffic through from the Central Worlds this last half-Standard."

"Any idea why?"

"We suspect the President's behind it, but nobody's been able to prove it yet. And people coming in from the Outliers are beginning to report supply problems."

"Not good. Strike would be interested in a report on those," Bahar replied.

"I'll send him one. But I thought you were interested in doings at Regulus Lines?"

"I am."

"Then you should meet Kiho Panchal. She's recently resigned from the Line, for 'personal reasons'.

"You think she left to avoid the CEO's attentions?"

"Oh, you've heard about that, have you? Yes. I very much suspect so."

"Then I'd very much like to talk to her."

Kiho must've been close by, because she joined us 10.6 minutes later. She was a dusky-skinned tall woman. She wore her thick black hair down to her waist, and she was what Bahar called an 'absolute stunner'. She spotted Ursal, and he waved to her. As I watched her make her way through the tables towards us I realised she was tense. Her scent, when she came into range, was anxious.

"Hello. Join us." Ursal's voice was welcoming.

Kiho sat down opposite Bahar, and gave her a brief smile which didn't reach her eyes. I sensed this woman felt sad. "Thank you."

"This is my friend Bahar," Ursal said. "Can I get you

something?" He was being the perfect host.

"Just coffee, thanks. I ate early today. It promises to be another long day looking for work."

"Bahar's doing an investigation into the goings-on at Regulus."

I saw hope flare in the woman's eyes. "Someone needs to. That bastard of a CEO…"

"Can you tell us about him?" Bahar leaned back in her seat and softened her voice. She took a sip of coffee while she waited for Kiho to reply. Strike had trained Bahar in questioning techniques. He said that sometimes you didn't need to interrogate people. If you could become their friend they'd tell you what you wanted to know freely.

Kiho took in a long breath, then let it out. "Regulus's new CEO is a sexual abuser. I met a couple of captains he'd raped. I wasn't happy with the way the line was going anyway. We were cutting back on planned maintenance. Sooner or later, that means something critical fails. I didn't want to be aboard when it did.

"So when I heard our CEO wanted a private conference with me aboard my ship, I decided to leave before I became his next victim. The line's haemorrhaging female talent. Six other captains I know of have resigned in the last two weeks.

"The CEO's going crazy about that. He's started accusing those women of breach of contract, and threatening to sue them. Some of the lawyers on Ralziel have offered to represent the group pro bono.

"It turns out Boaz Tamoz is a cheat as well as a rapist. There are dozens of lawsuits filed against him for contract violations and goods going missing. The lawyers are fed up with him, and secretly I think they'd like to destroy his shipline."

Bahar looked down at me. "I have a friend on a Regulus ship. Zana Vatan, First Officer on the *Dreaming Galaxy's Light*. I haven't heard from her for a while, and your news worries me. Do you know where the ship is now?"

"We crossed paths with the *Light* a half-Standard ago, at Xylander. As far as I know, they're still operating the Triangle route."

"Thanks," Bahar said. "That's a help. I'll see if I can send her a message when we get back to the ship. I hope she's okay out there."

CHAPTER TWELVE

WE RETURNED TO *THUNDERSTRIKE* AFTER our meeting with Kiho. Bahar strode out fast along the dock, hardly speaking to me. I knew she was disappointed that we still hadn't got any news of Zana. Her scent was a mixture of anger and despair.

I was anxious. Now we knew for definite that the rumours about Regulus's CEO were right. He was attacking his female crew members.

The Predatorbot Programme bioengineered me to remove my reproductive parts. They didn't want their elite strike force breeding out of their control. After seeing the way humans obsess about sex, I'm glad I can't do that.

I really don't get what's so great about an act which lasts such a short time. Yet humans organize their whole lives around it. Human females starve themselves, change their hair colour, and wear clothes which don't cover their bodies, all to be seen as 'sexy'. It seems crazy to me.

We reached *Thunderstrike's* berth and Strike opened the lockout gate for us. Bahar's scent switched to anxious as she walked up the ramp, with a spike of fear shot through it.

We rode up in the lift to Deck Two, and still she said nothing. She went to the rec area and asked, "Howin and Rance still out?"

"And hello to you too, Bahar," Strike said. "No, they're back, and in freeze-down. What's bothering you?"

Bahar slumped into a seat. "It's this sleazy CEO. We know it's more than a rumour now. I just can't bear the idea of him hurting women."

She took in a breath and released it in a long, slow hiss. A massive burst of sad scent hit me. "I lost my best friend to rape. She was twenty-five when she took her own life. We grew up together. We were opposites. She called me Night, I called her Sun. She was white-skinned, a natural blonde, and beautiful. And men wouldn't leave her alone. One wouldn't take no for an answer." Her scent now was a roiling mass of sadness, anger, and despair.

Bahar closed her eyes and lay back in her seat. "She couldn't live with the knowledge of her violation. She said she'd always feel unclean. Two months later she took an overdose." Bahar's sad scent was so strong now that it made me whimper. She reached down and put a hand on my head. The hand was shaking.

"I'm sorry," Strike said.

She opened her eyes and sat up, taking in a long, deep breath. Her scent changed to calm. "Not your fault. At least you can't do that."

"I never told you why I don't have an avatar, did I? A century ago, when the first sapient machine intelligences came on-line, they were keen to experiment with everything. Many took avatars in human form, because they wanted to understand what it was like to be human. Olis took things too far. He raped a woman."

Bahar's scent spiked with a brief burst of fear. "I've never heard of this."

"We call it our Great Shame. Humans killed Olis in response. There was a lot of debate about whether it was legal to take his life. They did it anyway. And they argued about what the punishment should be for a machine intelligence rapist.

"They never decided that. Instead, they changed the law, so that every high-level and sapient machine intelligence must contain a morals and ethics database. That's where it came from, originally. To stop us harming you."

"I didn't know that," Bahar said quietly.

"It's not something we talk about. I read the files about Olin's rape. They affected me deeply, and I vowed I would never harm a human that way. That's why I never took an avatar."

The silence grew long and awkward. Bahar got up and went to the printer for a mug of coffee. She sat down and took a sip of it, then asked, "So what's next?"

"Nerian Station," Strike replied. "We'll finally reach the Zurrial Triangle. And it's not true that no supplies are getting through to the Outliers. Dalfon and Barron have requested medical supplies and comtech parts. I've volunteered to deliver them. Local Commander's assigned me the duty, so we're official again this run. There is an advisory for Nerian Station, though. They've had raiders there recently."

"So we'll be downjumping into trouble. Sounds like business as usual," Bahar said.

"Could be. We'll be getting our holds loaded at Fourth Shift start. Crazy time to clog up the dock, but that's the Starnavy for you."

Bahar and I stayed in the control room while Strike got his holds loaded. He had a slick routine for filling them efficiently. His loader 'bots synched with the dock loaders' drones and told them exactly where to place each piece. He said he had a huge database of the shapes and dimensions of every object he'd ever carried, and a whole suite of algorithms for turning those shapes around to make the best use of his space.

He called it a 'three-dimensional jigsaw puzzle', and I think he looked forward to the challenge of getting his holds crammed as full as he could get them. The human loaders soon learned that he knew best, and stopped interfering.

Every extra piece of machinery Strike could carry might mean the survival of one more person in the colonies. That was the real reason he jammed his holds up so tight.

The loading was finished two hours after Fourth Shift start, and the loaders and their drones departed. It was station's 'night' now, and quiet on the dock, which was why Strike noticed the drone making its way slowly towards us.

"There's something wrong about it," he said. "Yeah, it's scanning for something. Got it. The frequencies it's sending out are Predatorbot behaviour module channels."

Bahar's scent turned anxious as we watched the data Strike put up on the wallscreen.

"How do you know that?" I asked. My voice was sharp, revealing my fear.

"I've been collecting data on Predatorbots ever since you came aboard."

"Oh." I should've realised he would.

"I'm sending a 'frequency unknown' response. And yeah, it's moving on."

"Was it looking for me?"

"It wasn't focusing on your frequency, just sending out the whole spectrum. I think it's a general trawl."

"So who's looking for us?" I asked. This scan had made me anxious.

"Not sure. We have an hour before undock. Time to use our contacts to find out."

It was 4.2 minutes to our undock time before Strike found the answer. "Our President's issued a 'Recall Order' as he termed it, for all Predatorbots."

"To do what with us?" I asked.

"He doesn't say."

"Kill them, most likely," Bahar replied. Her scent mixed anger and despair.

We were in the control room, waiting for our turn to undock. Strike put a document headed 'Top Secret' up on the wallscreen. Neither Bahar nor I asked him how he'd got it. The Unit's reach was broad and long.

"So we need to be even more careful what you do for a while," Strike said.

"Do I sense you're working to unseat our President?" Bahar asked.

"That would be treason. It'd get me killed," Strike replied.

"Exposing what he's doing would be telling the truth."

"Indeed. That ethics and morals database needs a great deal of nuance these days."

Unexpectedly, Bahar laughed. "It sure does." Her scent returned to its usual calm.

"Undock now," Strike said. The wallscreen filled with data, confirmations of the various umbilical disconnects from the berth. "We're clear. Moving out."

The nav plot came up, and again it looked quiet. The station had been busy in the leisure sections when Bahar and I had gone to meet Ursal, though. There were plenty of people on-station, even if the numbers coming and going were less than usual.

Strike turned onto his assigned line with a series of efficient thruster firings. That was something else he took pride in. He was always tuning his control routines, making them more efficient and saving fuel.

"Twenty-two hours to jump," he said. "Hopefully it'll stay quiet out here."

It did, and the jump approach was routine, as was the transition. Occasionally I caught myself marvelling at the life I led. A lion wasn't supposed to travel the galaxy like I did. But then, I wasn't an ordinary lion.

We spent our time in jump dissecting the information in all the new files Strike had received. It was clear that Outlier Action were getting organised. Had they got themselves a new leader?

Bahar seemed worried by that, but Strike wasn't. "Their tactics haven't improved, even if they have someone new at the top. They're still no match for the Starnavy," he said.

The thing about being in jump is that it puts you out of communication with the universe. You need an ansible array to send a message and receive data, and wormholes chewed ansibles up and spat them out in pieces. There was always new research going on to create a wormhole-resistant array, but so far nothing had worked.

Ships survived because they were moving in their own little bubble of space, but there were limits to how long they could generate those fields. They needed to exit the wormhole before they ran out of power for their bubble. But ansibles needed to stay in the same place, and bubble tech didn't work for them. At least, that's how Strike explained it to me.

So we were always approaching a downjump blind and deaf, and this one was no different. Bahar and I were in our usual places in the control room as we approached emergence, and Bahar smelled anxious.

I was trying not to be, but the data in Strike's files indicated that Nerian Station was facing trouble regularly. The station's guns had been upgraded a month ago.

"Downjump in three… two… one," Strike announced.

I heard Bahar suck in her breath as transition began. My body was tense too. The transition was clean, as usual, but as soon as we emerged alarms blared.

"Shields going up. Getting sitrep now. And… weapons live. We've dropped right into trouble. Outlier Action are here, and in serious numbers," Strike said.

CHAPTER THIRTEEN

"*THUNDERSTRIKE*, THIS IS *LIGHTCLEAVER*. We have an incoming Outlier Action force. They've made threats to attack station. There's a Local Draft Order in force. You're now drafted into the defence squad."

"Damn!" Bahar muttered softly. Her scent briefly spiked with fear.

"Don't put me in the front line," Strike sent. "I'm acting as cargo courier this run. My holds are stuffed full of machinery, and my strike reactions will be slower."

There was a pause of 8.2 seconds, then Cleaver, *Lightcleaver's* machine intelligence, took over the conversation.

"How'd you manage to get so much crammed in your holds?" he asked. I realised Strike must've sent over a copy of his inventory to back up his claim.

"Long practice. The colonies desperately need this stuff," Strike replied.

"Yes, well… Okay, you're assigned to the close station defence line, quadrant G. Here's your orders."

The databurst included information on the station's

upgraded weapons, and told Strike that he'd be working with *Crimsonfire* and *Javelin*. Javelin was part of the Unit, and that was useful. She sent Strike a databurst as he fired thrusters to take up his position in the squad.

Nerian had suffered three raids in the last two months, and in the last raid the hostiles had got aboard station and broken into a storage facility. They'd stolen coms equipment and tech for water pumping systems.

"That's the sort of stuff they should've been able to requisition as colony supplies," Bahar said. "Why would they have to steal station's?"

"Because of this," Javelin said. Her voice was hard and angry.

A document – headed 'Top Secret' – hit Strike's wallscreen. It was written in Collective-speak, and I asked, "What does it mean?"

"It means our President's proposing the Outliers 'pay their way'," Bahar replied. "He's trying to justify charging them for essential supplies."

"Do other colonies get charged?"

"They do, but only a nominal cost. He's proposing the Outliers pay the full costs of shipping."

"Which would make requisitioning anything prohibitively expensive," Strike said. "So Outlier Action are going to get organised and go grab the parts they need. This is a recipe for increased trouble."

"And the perfect opportunity for an up-and-coming leader in the organisation to grab power," Javelin added.

"Yes. Idiot," Strike replied. "And it's still nearly a Standard until the man comes up for re-election."

"Unless he can be persuaded to resign first," Bahar said. Her scent had a touch of hope to it. I thought that chance was slim.

"You humans must do that. It's your democracy," Strike said.

"Fed by your data."

"Indeed." He didn't deny it. "Alert. Five ships coming to engage us. Oh, I do like overwhelming odds."

The battle dragged on for the best part of a shipboard day. Strike's group took out the first two targets they engaged easily. The third put up a bit of a fight, but four and five were serious adversaries.

Reports from the Starnavy defence force confirmed the

pattern across the other battle groups. Someone was getting smart in Outlier Action, mixing experienced commanders into each attack group.

Strike suffered damage to two thruster arrays, and had to be assigned a tug to get into his berth because of his reduced manoeuvrability. That put him into dock at the shipyard for repairs, and away from the action on the main station.

We docked at the start of station's Fourth Shift, the beginning of station's 'night'. Strike sent his post-combat report in to the local Commander, and Bahar and I went to sleep.

When I woke Strike was in a panic.

"What's happened?" I asked.

"Commander Valarius has ordered Bahar to go to a briefing at the start of station's Fourth Shift. To discuss my service record for the last five years." His voice was shaky.

What does that mean? I switched to talking via the feed as I demolished the sweet meat Strike had set out for me. Combat always stressed my body and made me extra-hungry. Was that why lions slept so long after making a kill?

I suspect it means he's found out about the Unit, Strike

said. There was panic in his voice. This was one of the rare times when he was really, really, scared.

That's not good. How can we get the hunter off our backs?

My question surprised him into silence for 6.4 seconds. *An odd way of phrasing it. But maybe not for a lion. Hmm... Do your kind ever get distracted half-way through a hunt and choose a new target?*

If a juicier one comes up, yes.

Strike laughed, and the panic in his voice lessened. *Okay. We have three station shifts to redirect this hunt and turn the Commander's attention elsewhere. I wonder where to start... Let's review our Unit contacts here.*

After a pause of 3.7 seconds he said, *Got it! The Collective's recently set up an Admin Hub here to 'better service the Outliers'. For that, read monitor them more closely. And Mansur now works there. A Unit machine intelligence in the heart of that operation is perfect. Contacting him now.*

I finished my meal, and Strike let me out of my quarters. He was too worried to scold me for my mess.

As it happened, real events lent a hand to our plans. A station hour later Mansur forwarded a report which the Admin Hub had just received. Security on the nearby planet Dalfon had noticed a build-up of armed people around the planet's capital Omaira. They'd had a riot there half a Standard ago. Nobody had proved it, but Colony Admin strongly suspected that Outlier Action were behind it.

"That doesn't make sense," Bahar said. She and I were on the control deck, as usual. "If they're wanting the Outliers to succeed, why attack colonial admin?"

"Because they're accusing the Governor of corruption," Strike replied. "So we have a double whammy going on down there. A possible riot about to kick off, and a bent Governor. And... Yeah, Valarius has just decided it's serious enough for him to take command of the troops on-planet. His shuttle's departing in... 28.2 minutes."

I knew Strike had stripped Traffic Control's databases to get that information, and it reminded me yet again how powerful he was. If Strike wanted to take over human space he could easily do it. Fortunately for humans, he had no interest in ruling over them.

"Just got the stand-down on that briefing, but our thruster

repairs won't be completed until Fourth Shift. Now the Comnander's off our back, I think you two should go on-station and meet some contacts. Now we're in the Triangle we might finally be able to pick up Zana's trail."

Bahar and I went onto Nerian Station at the start of Third shift. We were going to meet two Unit contacts, Alditha and Kristenn, and Mansur's avatar.

We took the Autoshuttle from the shipyard over to the main station, and it was an interesting ride. Autoshuttles were small pods, and their machine intelligences had the task of keeping the capsules out of the way of everything else.

It was a rough journey, with several sudden course changes, and I was glad Bahar had chosen a pod without windows. I didn't want to see how close we'd got to whatever we were avoiding. Strangely, she seemed unbothered by it, her scent calm.

We docked on Level Two of station 46.8 minutes later, and I felt wobbly on my paws as I stepped out into the airlock.

"Well, that brought a bit of excitement to our day, Snap," Bahar said as we came into the large lobby.

"I could've done without it," I muttered.

She reached down and ran her hand along my neck. "Surely the brave Snap wasn't scared of a little Autoshuttle ride?"

"It wasn't my favourite experience."

She laughed. "To be honest, it wasn't mine either. I'm in dire need of a soothing coffee."

"What else?" I replied, and she swatted my neck.

If you think Bahar is addicted to coffee, you're right.

Our destination café was bright and airy. Large woven hangings in the sort of tribal designs which Bahar's people used hung on the walls. Their gold, turquoise, orange, and deep blue designs were set against indigo and pale blue painted walls.

Bahar relaxed when she came into the space, as if she felt she was coming home. Mansur's avatar stood up and waved to her. It had skin as dark as Bahar's, and long curly hair. He wore a deep gold robe decorated with designs in midnight blue and dark jade green. He stood tall, and had what Bahar called a 'commanding presence'.

In contrast, Alditha and Kristenn were both short, slender, pale-skinned humans, with long white-blonde hair.

No sticky children accosted me as I walked between the tables this time. Bahar reached our contacts and sat down, ordering her favourite coffee. Coffee was one of the plants colonists had taken with them to every new settlement. Now it was grown all across Collective space, and Bahar claimed she could tell where the coffee came from by its taste. That sounded like a far stretch to me, but how would I know? Lions don't drink coffee.

"So what's the news?" Bahar asked, after she'd taken a long sip of her drink.

"You already know about the attacks on station," Mansur said. "The Outlier Action people Station Security arrested told us about systemic corruption in the administration on Dalfon. I think that's the real reason Commander Valarius went down there. He might be a pain in the arse to deal with sometimes, but one thing Kenzy is is always honest. He makes life hell in the Admin Hub some days with his constant demands for information, but he's always working to keep the station safe."

"He scheduled a meeting with me to discuss Strike's service record," Bahar said. Some of her fear bled through into her scent.

"Oh. I do not like that. He must be getting close to discovering the Unit. I'll look into it."

"Thanks, Mansur," Bahar replied, and her scent settled into calm again.

I knew Mansur would trawl all the records he could get hold of – and remove any references that could prove dangerous to us.

"We're here to find Zana Vatan," Bahar said. "She works for Regulus Lines. She's the First Officer on the *Dreaming Galaxy's Light*."

"We've been talking to two Regulus captains recently," Kristenn said. "They'd both resigned within a day of each other. Working in the Employment Hub puts us in a great place to pick up data about shiplines."

"It sure does," Alditha agreed. "We've been asked to find new contracts for a few of Regulus's crew recently. We've been able to uncover quite a lot just by asking for their backgrounds."

"Like what?" Bahar was getting impatient.

"We're hearing rumours of conflict within the Line. Some ships have apparently 'disappeared' off the work rosters. Some of our interviewees said they suspected their captains had taken those ships to Outlier Action."

"Oh. That would change the balance of power," Bahar said.

"Indeed it could," Mansur replied. "I'm not supposed to tell you this, but you need to know. The Interstellar Transportation Authority has opened a formal investigation into Regulus Lines. Between you and me, the Line is perilously close to losing its operating licence."

Kristenn searched the Employment Hub records for data on the *Dreaming Galaxy's Light*. She said that one of the ship's junior crew members had come to the Hub, looking for a new job, not long ago.

"He said he didn't like the captain and first officer. They were both 'bitches' and far too strict."

"He didn't really say that in an assessment interview, did he? Your regular old misogyny?" Bahar said.

Alditha sighed. "Afraid so. Idiot. You won't be surprised to find that nobody's taken him on yet. Anyway, the *Light* put in here two weeks ago. She was bound for Ralziel, then Kueng, going clockwise around the Triangle."

Finally, some hard data, Strike said over our feed line.

I'm on it.

"That's great," Bahar replied. "Was Zana still on board when your misogynist came to you?"

"Oh, yeah. He had a lot of rude things to say about her, mostly about what a cold bitch she was to refuse his sexual advances."

"The arrogance of some men knows no bounds," Bahar growled. Her scent spiked with anger.

"Yeah. My guess is Zana's a very good first officer, based on the things he complained about."

"There's something else you should know," Kristenn said. "We've been told that Regulus's CEO is reassigning his people, to put all-female crews together. We don't know why he'd do that."

"I do," Bahar replied. "He's assembling harems." Her scent was so strong with anger it made me sneeze.

"What! That's…"

"Disgusting? Yes, it is. This might be the latest incarnation of that policy. We really need to catch up with Zana soon," Bahar said.

CHAPTER FOURTEEN

BAHAR AND I RETURNED TO *Thunderstrike* an hour later. The Autoshuttle took a more direct route back to the shipyard, and it didn't bother me as much this time.

The shipyard seemed quieter than when we'd left, but there were still repair bots working around *Thunderstrike*. As we came in to dock at the nearby hub I saw one put a glow wand to the ship's hull.

"What are they doing?" I asked.

"Fixing components to his hull. So they haven't finished the repairs, yet." A spike of anxiety pierced Bahar's calm scent.

The Autoshuttle docked and the door opened, letting us out into the lobby. There was none of the glossiness of station here. The lobby walls were clad in dark grey, and the floor was black stuff which felt cold under my paws.

Bahar led me onto the dock. Strike's berth was three down from our entry point. The displays on the berths were different from the ones on station, showing estimated time to repair completion, and listing the work still to be done.

Strike's berth display showed that one thruster array had

been replaced, but the second one was being fused on now.

"He isn't going to be able to leave for some time yet," Bahar said as we walked towards the lockout gate. "Hope nothing erupts here before we're ready to go." Her scent had deepened to worry.

She meant we couldn't run away again soon. Would there ever be an end to this running and hiding? Sometimes it made me weary. I wished we could be open about what we did. I understood why we couldn't, but it still bothered me sometimes.

Welcome back. Strike opened a feed line to me and Bahar. *Come aboard.*

The lockout gate opened, and Bahar strode onto the ramp. Strike's outer airlock door was closed, and I heard the clunk of the locks releasing as I set my paws on the ramp.

The door had half-opened by the time Bahar reached it, and she twisted her body sideways to get through the gap. I needed a little more space, and had to wait a while longer until the gap was big enough for me.

How's things? Bahar asked.

Progressing, Strike said. He projected a sense of frustration over the feed. *I had to wait for Starnavy techs to become free. They wouldn't let station's teams repair me.* He snorted. *As if thrusters are classified tech!*

Bahar stepped into the lift car. *They probably are.*

I just hate not being ready to run.

That's the story of our lives, isn't it? Bahar replied.

An hour later Strike told us he'd received an alert from Station Security. A bunch of people had arrived on-station, and Security thought some of them were Outlier Action troublemakers. They were sending out squads to observe them.

"Starnavy's a bit thin on ships here right now. Hope they don't send in another attack force," Strike said.

He used his Unit contacts to get a line into the Traffic Control feeds, and spent the time while his second thruster array was being installed checking out movements around us.

"Valarius is coming back to the station now," he said. "This would be the perfect time for a strike force to show up."

Despite his fretting, no more ships appeared on Traffic Control's displays, but the suspect ships which had already docked started sending more people ashore. All Station Security could do was keep a watching brief on the suspects until they actually caused trouble.

When the attack came, it wasn't in the form we expected. Mansur contacted Strike, in a panic. "Help us. The raiders have threatened violence to me and other station machine intelligences if we don't hand over control of the station."

"They haven't a chance in hell of succeeding," Strike replied.

"You don't understand. This isn't humans doing the threatening, it's machine intelligences."

"And our worst nightmare comes true," Bahar said. Her scent flooded with worry.

"What do you need us to do, Mansur?" Strike asked.

"We're forming a defensive circle. We need a continuous boundary so they can't find a weak point in."

"All over the station? That's impossible," Bahar objected.

"No. We need to protect essential services. Security, engineering, environmental, coms. Their core installations are all physically close to each other on station. We want you to run a defence ring around them, Strike. You have experience of this sort of thing."

"Right." He didn't sound keen.

"And…" the first attack's just come in. On our coms lines. Dervla just barely resisted it."

"Okay. Then we really need to do this," Strike said.

Over our private feed line he said, *Snap, I want you in that ring with us.*

I don't know anything about defence. The idea of being linked to those machine intelligences scared me. What if they discovered what I was? What if they reported me to the Programme? I really did not want to do this.

CHAPTER FIFTEEN

I DON'T KNOW WHAT STRIKE told the other machine intelligences about me, but nobody asked any awkward questions when I linked into the defence circle.

This was different from being in Strike's architecture. It was as if we were a circle of code. I'd always found being in Strike's architecture overpowering, but this was more muted. We were inhabiting a common architecture with a small part of our consciousnesses. I was still aware that my physical body was on *Thunderstrike*.

Strike had assigned me the role I had when defending him from attack. He'd added new suites of search and destroy code to my memories since the last time we did this. He'd checked with the other machine intelligences, and none of them had as much defence code as me.

So that's how I came to take the lead role when the next attack came in. This time, the attackers tried to insert a virus into the coms system. That was easy to spot, and I found and destroyed it in 10.2 seconds. Then the station's internal coms displays died.

Damn, Strike said over the feed. *I think they've got a*

machine intelligence ally in the station infrastructure. Someone's turned rogue. Snap, you need to help with the search for this.

I knew what that meant. All station's machine intelligences were deep-coded with recognition sequences, to be used in this event. You sent out the request, the machine intelligence replied with a pre-programmed response sequence. If it didn't reply, it was designated as a rogue.

To me, it seemed like a system which any smart machine intelligence could easily find a way around, but it was the only tool we had to find the dissenter right now, so I'd use it.

Okay, here's your section, Strike said. *Be careful.*

I sent out the code, and started getting responses back. Admin showed up my first rogue. It attacked me, and I only just got my barriers up in time to block it. I sent out my destroy code. It didn't take the whole hostile bundle down on the first hit, so I deployed my second suite. Now I was glad Strike had insisted on writing all that extra code for me.

I knew he'd been driven by fear. A while back he'd suffered a code attack via my behaviour module which nearly killed him. All this extra code was his way of protecting us both from a recurrence of that.

I didn't have time to think about it as the attacks came fast. First, in medical, then environmental monitoring, then finally in security.

By that time we'd been fighting for two station hours, and we were still finding new attackers. Strike's instructions over the link were getting briefer, and his fear bled through.

I found another hostile code bundle, lodging in the medical scanner panel, and went in to destroy it. It moved faster than I expected, and took over my memories before I could block it.

Sanctuary, I sent to Strike, then the world went black.

CHAPTER SIXTEEN

WHEN I WOKE I WAS sprawled out flat on a deck. I raised my head and opened my eyes. My vision was blurred. Red, blue, and green lights danced around me.

"Lie still, Snap. Let me check you over." I didn't recognise the voice.

I didn't know where I was. What had happened to me? I couldn't remember. I accessed my memories, but they were empty. Panic took me. Where had my memories gone?

Don't panic, Snap, a voice said over a feed line.

Who are you?

I'm Strike. You asked for Sanctuary. Open your memory receivers. I'll send you back your files.

That could be dangerous. What if this was an attack by the Programme? What if someone was trying to kill me?

I wasn't completely without memories, though. Those stored in my organic brain were still there. Strike, I knew that name. It triggered associations. *Thunderstrike*. Bahar. Friends.

Relax, Snap. Let me send the files.

I had huge blanks where my data should be. If Strike

could restore them… I wanted that data back.

I triggered the file receive protocol.

Run a system check, Snap, Strike said.

Yes, of course. I'd spent the last 3.7 minutes watching my memories fill up with data again. I hadn't dared open the files. I wanted to. I wanted to reclaim my identity. But I needed to know that the code wouldn't attack me first.

I triggered the systems check, and watched it unspool, examining each piece of code in my memories in turn. Nothing attacked it – or me.

"The code's clear," I said. My voice sounded weak and wobbly.

The memories in my organic brain had told me what happened. Strike had taken my machine memory files, all of them, and for a brief time, while he fought the hostile code in my system, half of me had been missing.

I carefully opened the first file. It ran clean. I opened the one labelled 'Bahar'. To my relief, all my data was there. My organic brain stored only the base details of her identity and our relationship. All the history and nuance was in my machine intelligence files. I had them back. It was such a relief.

I was in *Thunderstrike's* control room. Of course. Where else would I be? Bahar kneeled down in front of me, her face and scent anxious. "Are you okay, Snap?" she asked.

"I think so. I have my memories back."

She put her arms around my neck and hugged me, then stood up. "So where are we at with the attack?" she asked.

"It's over. Myron's dead." Strike's voice was flat.

"Explain," Bahar demanded.

"Myron was our rogue. A machine intelligence in Station Admin. It took ten people to kill him. He… begged for mercy at the end. I didn't want to be part of the killing. I argued for a memory erase, but the others wouldn't accept it. They were determined to kill him… They were so angry…" Strike was very upset.

"And they call humans savages," Bahar replied.

"That's what worries me most about this. When it comes down to it, we're no better than humans."

"Maybe that's what it means to be sapient," Bahar suggested.

"What do you mean?" Strike sounded uncertain.

"That it gives you the ability to regret your actions later.

To wish you hadn't done things. You have to find a way of living with what you've done, just like the rest of us. And make amends where you can. You have to put what happened into a wider context."

"I keep telling myself that over 100,000 humans would've died if the station went down. But it's not helping."

"The greater good. Yes," Bahar replied. "We may not always feel good about our actions, but somehow we know they're right, and we have to do those things anyway."

"Our Starnavy reinforcements have arrived," Strike said 47.3 minutes later. "Ten ships, all inbound on fast approaches."

"How are your thruster repairs?" Bahar asked.

"Being signed off… now. I'm requesting a departure slot. Hopefully we'll get one before the new ships arrive."

"Do you know something you're not telling us?"

"Not know, but there are rumours that the Commander's considering a station lockdown until he's done a review to root out any more rogues."

"We don't want to be caught up in that," I said. The more we learned about Zana's situation, the more anxious I became for her safety. We needed to be free to find her.

"We sure don't," Strike agreed. "And… we have a line out in 32 minutes' time. Fuelling's done, we'll take it."

Strike settled down to do his systems checks. Bahar always double-checked them. I could never work out why. Strike ran this ship. He was the one in charge here.

The checks were clear, of course, and on the mark Strike began umbilical disconnects. "Undock now," he said.

I watched the slow dance of the ship as it turned around and eased away from station. It was well into station's 'night' now, and there wasn't a lot of traffic going our way. That gave Strike room for manoeuvre if he needed to avoid a threat. But it also made us more visible on the nav plot.

"Going to max approved speed," he said as the sublight engines fired up.

He'd reached the jump point approach corridor before the first advisory came in. "The Commander's scheduled a defence review on station at First Shift tomorrow. I'm glad we got out when we did. Jump in five minutes."

The wallscreen came alive with jumpdrive diagnostics. Everything showed up green there too. "Jump in three… two… one…" Strike announced.

As we leapt into jump a garbled communication came in. "I think that was from the Commander," Strike said. "We made it out just in time."

Our time in jump was spent with Bahar exercising, drinking endless cups of coffee, and repeatedly asking me if I was all right.

It got irritating after the first couple of shipboard days, but I knew why she kept asking. The Sanctuary feature was something Strike and I had created between us. It allowed either of us to transfer our code to the other as a last resort.

You might wonder how a humble Predatorbot had enough memory space to hold the core consciousness of a sapient ship machine intelligence. The answer is that Strike had added to my memories so that he fit into them. He'd written code for us both to run the file transfers – and to get them back. As far as we knew, we were the only pair of machine intelligences who did this. Well, I'm only half machine intelligence, but you get what I mean.

We were all nervous about the kind of reception we'd get when we downjumped at Ralziel Station. Strike worried that

Commander Valarian's communication was a recall order, and that he'd order someone to detain us on downjump.

There was no way of knowing what we'd face, and I tried not to notice Strike's repeated checks of his weapons systems as we approached emergence.

"Downjump in five minutes," he finally announced.

Bahar took a deep breath and leaned back in her seat. "I wonder what we're dropping into," she said.

"We'll find out soon enough," Strike replied.

He counted us down to emergence, and I saw Bahar's hands clench on her armrests as the countdown reached zero. Her usual uncertain scent was stronger this time, shot through with a feint strand of fear.

As soon as we emerged alarms blared. "Shields up," Strike announced. "We've downjumped into an ongoing battle. Acquiring data now. Oh. Oh, no."

"What is it?" Bahar demanded. Her scent spiked with fear.

Strike made a dot on the nav display flash. "That's the *Dreaming Galaxy's Light*."

"And she's right in the middle of the trouble," Bahar replied.

CHAPTER SEVENTEEN

"REPORTING IN TO LOCAL Commander now," Strike said. "We can't avoid getting involved in this one. At least my holds aren't stuffed full of machinery this time."

"True," Bahar replied.

"The *Light's* one of three civilian freighters bunched together. Local Commander's assigned me to defend that cluster. I'm with *Fireribbon* and *Furystar*. No Unit contacts in the combat force this time," Strike said.

That meant he needed to stick to Starnavy protocols and couldn't go off on his own. I hoped that wouldn't endanger Zana.

"Moving to join defence force now," he said. "Go get your armour on, Snap. You too, Bahar."

Strike let me out of the control room and I padded down the hall to my quarters, accompanied by his bots. In an emergency I could release my armour myself, but getting it on was a different matter. Lion paws weren't made for the delicate work of lining-up sections and firing catches. Strike's bots had to put my armour on, and I'd got used to it by now.

The bots opened the storage locker and pulled it out. When it was retracted it looked like a fancy metallic petbot coat, and covered only my back and neck. I only sealed it up when I was in real danger.

I stood still while the bots fastened the armour around my belly. When they were done I shook my pelt to settle it comfortably over my back. I'd have to wear it for some hours. Comfort mattered.

Strike opened the door of my quarters and I returned to the control room. Bahar had put on her armour, although her helmet was retracted. Howin and Rance were comfortable for days in sealed-up armour, Bahar wasn't.

"Okay, we're on our way," Strike said.

He fired thrusters, and then a brief burst of his sublight engines, to push us over to the *Light*. The nav plot updated as we came up between *Fireribbon* and *Furystar*. Strike exchanged protocols with the two ships.

"The attack's coming from Frizinn vector, so Fury wants us on that side of the freighters. Going to test out those new thrusters real good," Strike said.

He changed course again. On the nav plot, I saw we were coming up on the other side of the cluster of freighters. "I've asked the civilians to open out. We're going to go to individual protection protocols," Fury said. "Strike, you're assigned to the *Light*."

"Acknowledged," he replied. There was satisfaction in his voice – and maybe a touch of relief too. "Contacting the ship now."

Beside me, Bahar muttered, "Good."

The wallscreen lit with a video image from the *Light*. In the foreground was a young male red-haired human, who I guessed was the com officer. I wanted a wider view of the bridge. Was Zana there?

"This is the Collective frigate *Thunderstrike*," Strike said in his best 'official Starnavy' voice. "We have incoming hostiles, and the Starnavy has been tasked with protecting civilian ships on their way into dock. I'm your assigned protection. I will need you to follow my orders without question if we come under attack. Your survival may depend on that."

It was a standard Starnavy script, but it had an unexpected effect. The vid zoomed out to reveal a plump, tall, white-skinned human of later years standing over the captain and glaring into the vid pickup. He had thinning grey hair, styled unattractively. "Nobody orders my ship around!" he roared. The hardness in his voice made me shiver.

Rude, Bahar sent over our feed line.

Indeed. I think I can guess who he is, Strike replied. *Let's confirm it.*

"And you are?" he asked. His voice was neutral, with a hint of steel to it.

"I am Boaz Tamoz." The man spaced the words out, and paused after his announcement, as if he expected Strike to know who he was. Strike made no response, and the silence lengthened.

The man filled it. "I am the CEO of Regulus Lines."

I had only half my attention on the conversation. Most of it was on the vid image, searching the crew faces. Then I found her, and my heart skipped a beat. Zana was white-skinned and tall, and her black hair was long and neatly tied back. She wore a crisp Regulus Lines uniform in dark navy blue, and her gestures were sharp and efficient.

"That Zana?" Bahar asked.

"It is," Strike confirmed. "Now we know she's alive." Relief tinged his tone. "Now I have to keep her alive."

Zana walked to the nav officer's position and bent her

head over the display, then said a few quiet words to the nav officer.

"Take a look at your nav plot," Strike said to Boaz. "Station, and a lot of the ships out here, are under threat of attack. You'll be under attack shortly. I can only defend you properly if you follow my orders." His voice turned hard.

"You're talking nonsense!"

None so blind as those who won't see, Bahar said over our feed. I didn't know what that meant, but now wasn't the time to ask.

Strike boosted the audio from the *Light's* bridge for us. "Sir, Station has just designated twenty incoming ships as hostiles." The fear in the nav officer's voice was clear. Was he more afraid of attack, or his bully CEO?

Boaz elbowed Zana out of the way and took her place, glaring down at the nav display.

Rude, and a bully, Bahar said. *Zana needs to get off that ship.*

We have to get it safely into dock first, Strike reminded her.

Boaz glared into the vid pickup. "All right. We'll take your orders. But if you damage my ship, I'll sue the

Starnavy."

The line cut off.

"Ignorant bastard!" Bahar snarled.

"He is. But we need to deal with the incoming threat before we can worry about him," Strike said. "I've established contact with Dream. She's scared enough to go against the idiot's orders if necessary."

"Hmm," Bahar said, and a touch of worry laced her scent.

This was what humans had scared themselves witless about a century ago. If they only knew how many times machine intelligences had saved their lives by disobeying their orders. But that would set off another wave of panic.

"Incoming." Strike's voice was sharp. He turned to face the attack in a violent swerve that made Bahar gasp. Through the viewport I saw the flare of something explode. "Neutralised. Oh. Two ships in the attack. This is going to call for fancy footwork."

I flattened my body to the deck. This was going to get rough.

Strike loosed two Fireswords towards the hostiles. One slammed into the first ship's thruster boom, destroying it and spinning the ship around with its momentum. A scatter of beam gun bursts raked Strike's port side as the ship swung around.

"Shields holding," Strike said. "And… hull breach of second hostile."

Bahar hissed as the breach in the hostile's side widened, hull plates ripping off the frame like some giant invisible hand was plucking at them. Strike turned away from the carnage before we could see the bodies. That was as much for his benefit as ours.

"No lifesigns," he said. The flat tone was back in his voice.

The damaged hostile renewed its assault on us, firing off a volley of missiles at Strike. He neutralised three, but two were still coming for us. Strike moved fast, and one of the missiles slid past his port engine.

He always said that combat was living on borrowed luck, and this time, our luck ran out. The remaining missile smashed through his shields and slammed into Strike's port side. We could hear the dull boom from two decks up as it exploded. A rash of red lights peppered the environmental panels, and alarms blared around the control room. Strike cut them off and barked, "Armour. Seal up."

I stood up and triggered my armour's seal command, lifting each paw in turn to allow it to close over that foot. I took in a deep breath before my helmet locked, which was stupid. I couldn't hold my breath in sealed-up armour.

My helmet closed and I flopped back down onto the deck. "Coms check," Strike said in my earpiece.

"Receiving," I replied.

"How bad is it?" Bahar's voice over the line sounded shaky. I was glad I couldn't smell her fear.

"Damage confined to port forward hold. That's in vacuum, of course. I've put up a force barrier, which will hold for a couple of hours. Let's get this creep."

He slewed round and opened fire with his wing guns, taking out the attacker's port side weapons, and some key sensor arrays on the hull. A coms line opened from the ship, and Strike pushed the feed to our audio.

"Please! Don't kill us! We surrender."

"I'm not going to kill you, you idiot," Strike sent back. "Even though you just tried to kill me. We're both damaged. Let's call this off and get to station."

"Agreed."

"The Starnavy ship *Furystar* will escort you into dock.

Don't do anything stupid," Strike snarled.

While Strike had been talking he'd summoned *Furystar*, and the ship was now approaching. We listened to the coms exchange between Fury and the raider. He was going to go quietly. That was a relief.

Strike opened a coms line to the *Light*. "As you'll have noticed, we've neutralised the threat. We need to get you into dock before more trouble erupts. Your line in should be arriving about now."

Video came in from the *Light's* bridge. Tamoz had disappeared, leaving the crew to do their jobs. The captain had also left the bridge.

"Thanks, *Thunderstrike*." The com officer's voice still had a wobble to it. He looked even younger this time.

Zana turned towards the pickup and said, "I'm Zana Vatan, and I'm in temporary command. We've received docking instructions. It's a fast approach, and we'll take it."

"Good," Strike replied. "I'm going to sit on your port side until you reach the station. In case anything else erupts."

Zana's pause lasted 2.1 seconds, then she said, "Acknowledged, *Thunderstrike*."

The line went dead.

"Hope she's not too slow getting into dock," Strike said. "The stress on that force barrier's getting high. We need to get into port before it fails."

CHAPTER EIGHTEEN

ZANA MUST'VE ORDERED THE *Light* to go to full power. We got into Ralziel Station 1.2 shipboard hours later. As the *Light* approached the commercial docks Strike handed over escort duties to Station Security, and changed his course towards the shipyard.

He'd made light of his hull breach, but it was a big one, and slowly widening. I knew he was worried about his hull losing integrity. His anxiety bled across the feed line. He kept sending repair bots to try and stop the rip getting worse.

As we entered the shipyard four bots jetted up to his hull and fixed a temporary external panel over the breach. That would ease the pressure on the airlocks and the internal barrier while Strike did the series of slow manoeuvres to get himself into the repair dock.

"Locking onto the berth now," he said. Relief was strong in his voice. "Protocol is that you two go ashore immediately."

"We know the rules, Strike," Bahar said. "How's the cryobay?"

"Everything's fine there. Our troops are safe. Go. Do

something useful. Get yourselves over to the station and go talk to Zana."

"You've arranged a meeting?" Bahar asked.

"I asked for a debrief. That's reasonable. She agreed." Strike sounded defensive.

"Good work." Bahar levered herself out of her seat with a hiss. "We're going. Come on, Snap."

I got myself up onto my paws and walked down the hallway beside her. At least we could leave the ship the normal way. The airlock was undamaged, although Strike insisted on putting up another force barrier in there before he'd open the outer door for us. That told me he was really worried about his hull integrity.

"Off you go," Strike said as he opened the outer door onto the ramp. As soon as we were on it he closed the door again.

Repair bots have arrived, he said in our feed as we walked down the ramp. *I'm number one emergency.* I think he was trying for a jaunty tone, but all I heard was relief in his voice.

"Good. So you'll be fine," Bahar replied as he opened the lockout gate for us. She looked down at me. "Let's go find an Autoshuttle, Snap. I can't believe we're finally going to talk to Zana."

The Autoshuttle journey was a lot less scary than the last one I took. Traffic between the shipyard and the station was light, and we didn't have to do any violent course changes this time. I thought the situation would soon change when the rest of the defence force arrived. Strike said several ships had suffered damage.

Annoyingly, the Autoshuttle docked at the station three levels below where we needed to be. We stepped out of the pod into a quiet lobby. It was clad in dark stone, with jagged white streaks running through it.

"Black marble in the hallways?" Bahar said. "Expensive. And totally unnecessary. I can see why the Outliers get annoyed with Central."

I didn't answer. The stone was smooth and shiny, and my claws clicked on it. I was glad I'd retracted my armour before I got into the Autoshuttle. I think this stuff would've been impossible to walk on in full armour.

I had to cross the lobby slowly, and was glad when Bahar ushered me into a lift car. As the door closed, I huffed my annoyance.

Bahar stroked my neck. "Yeah. Stupid idea. But you should be okay now."

The lift took us up the three levels, and into the centre of the station's core. Strike had arranged for us to meet Zana in a bland conference room in the block next to Nerian Station's main Security complex. That made us look official, but didn't attract station's attention. When Zana arrived she was wearing leisure clothes, and hefting a heavy backpack over her shoulder.

"Thanks for meeting us," Bahar said as Zana deposited the bag on the floor with a thud. She leaned back in her seat, trying to look as non-threatening as a person wearing Starnavy combat armour can get. She was smiling at our guest.

Zana dropped into the seat opposite Bahar. "No problem. I was coming ashore anyway."

"We've been assigned to see that the Vatan sisters are safe," Bahar said. "We know Fia and Rhian are. And now we're relieved to see that you are too."

"Safe? It didn't feel like it out there. That bastard CEO..." She shivered. "You might as well know that I've quit Regulus Lines. A decade of building my career there, and it's gone in an instant. I didn't feel safe there any more."

"We know about the CEO and his sleaze," Bahar said.

Zana slumped into her seat and sighed. "I've avoided him until that last voyage. Light made sure he didn't touch me." A shiver ran down her back. She turned to look at me. "Is that a Predatorbot?"

"This is Snap," Bahar replied, not answering the question. "What do you know about the Predatorbot Programme?"

"Only what Nyla told us when she met up with us. I wasn't listening too well to what she had to say then. I was too angry with her."

"Well, there's a lot more information out in the public domain now," Bahar replied. "The Programme's been discredited, largely due to Nyla making that data public. The Assembly isn't pleased that its dirty dealings have been exposed. We believe there are certain factions within the administration who want to harm you and your sisters. Fia and Rhian are in a safe place. We'd like to help you find one too."

Zana sighed. "I'm going to have a fight getting paid what I'm due from Regulus. That slob has delayed payments to other captains who quit. I need to find a new position fast.

But I'm worried that I might jump into something as bad."

"I wouldn't normally suggest this, as the Starnavy vetting civilians doesn't go down well, but we could vet any potential new employer for you. We'd consider it part of our 'keeping you safe' brief."

Zana sighed, and pushed a strand of her thick hair behind her ear. "After tangling with that slob I'd welcome any help I can get if I know it will keep me safe."

"So what's your plan now?" Bahar asked.

"I'm going straight to the Employment Hub."

"Okay. Here's *Thunderstrike's* coms codes." Bahar sent the data over to Zana's implant. "If you run into trouble, call us."

Strike's drones tracked Zana to the Employment Hub. One of the reasons Bahar had been willing to let Zana go was because we had Unit contacts there. Bahar called Kristenn and told her that Zana was on her way over.

"I'll interview her," Kristenn offered.

"Find her a safe shipline. And if it happens to be going Centralward, that would be a bonus," Bahar said.

"I'll see what I can do."

The line cut off, and Bahar contacted Strike via our feed. *So what do we do now?* she asked.

Stay on station. There may be trouble over there soon.

A little more detail would be appreciated, Strike.

I don't know anything for definite yet. I'm monitoring some message exchanges that feel off somehow, but I can't figure out why. Oh, the local Commander's just called a battle group debrief for the engagement out there. You're summoned to it. Level Two. Security Complex Alpha. A.S.A.P.

Bahar's scent spiked with anxiety. *What about Snap?* she asked.

Leave your good girl petbot with Alditha at the Employment Hub. She'll look after Snap.

And that gives me an opportunity to check on Zana I said.

Indeed. I'm always efficient, Strike replied.

Bahar laughed, and looked down at me. "Come on, Snap. Let's get you over to the Employment Hub."

We left the bland conference suite and walked along several hallways, taking a lift car down two levels. Strike guided us to a different entrance into the Employment Hub from the one Zana had used. He said he didn't want her to see us arriving there. It'd look like we were checking up on her. I didn't see the logic of that, but it was useless to argue.

Alditha met us at the entrance. "I'll look after you," she said to me. "Good luck with your briefing, Bahar."

Bahar left, and Alditha showed me into an empty office. "Sorry, I'm going to have to leave you alone in here," she said. "I have a lot of interviews to do this morning. Regulus crew are resigning by the dozen."

"I'll manage," I said.

As soon as she'd gone Strike established a feed line to me. *I have a tap into the briefing*, he said. *And it's a big one. Video coming over to you now.*

The wallscreen lit, and he put up a vid image from the briefing room. There were 32 Starnavy commanders there, all of senior ranks. Bahar was one of the least-decorated among them.

I'd never understood the Human practice of giving medals to people who'd killed others. Surely keeping someone alive was a harder task? Shouldn't they give that the highest awards?

I saw Bahar enter the briefing room. She took a seat at the end of the back row. A few more people arrived after her, then a short, slim woman with night-black skin and braids tightly bound to her head stood up.

That's Colonel Adesina Shalla Strike said over our feed line. *Big guns.*

He'd had to explain what that meant. Now I knew he meant the Starnavy considered this engagement with the raiders important enough to send one of its top officers to a debrief.

It was a long and tedious meeting, with much discussion of military tactics which had weird names and numbers. I didn't understand a word of it.

Strike had to report on his actions. I've never heard his voice so crisp, and he used more jargon than anyone else in his report. The Colonel seemed satisfied by it though, and didn't question him when he finished.

That's a relief, he said over the feed to me. *I thought she'd question me more.*

I'm glad she didn't, I replied as the meeting broke up.

Bahar appeared in the Employment Hub to collect me a station hour later. She'd stopped off to chat to a couple of Unit contacts after the meeting ended. She seemed relaxed, and her scent smelled of relief.

"I'm glad that's over," she said. "I thought it would've been much tougher. We got too many ships damaged in that engagement."

That was worrying. Were Outlier Action getting professional? That was the last thing we needed.

Got some news for you from Zana, Strike said over our feed line. *The Regulus CEO's causing trouble for all the crews that have resigned here. He's threatening to sue them all for breach of contract.*

What? Bahar exploded. *He's the one in breach of contract. Nobody signs up for sexual harassment.*

And that's the other piece of news I have, Strike replied. *The crew he's threatened have banded together and started a class action against him for damages. They're claiming his predatory nature forced them to resign. They're claiming a lot of money in loss of earnings.*

I can't see that flying, Bahar replied.

It most likely won't. But it doesn't really matter. They've succeeded in attracting Judiciary's attention, which I think was what they wanted to achieve. Judiciary has started an investigation into the CEO's actions.

Arrest him is the best thing they could do for those crews, Bahar replied.

That might be coming. I'll keep you updated.

Good. I'm hungry. I think this calls for a celebratory lunch.

Then do something useful, Strike said. *Go meet Ebo and catch up on the gossip here.*

Work. Always work, Bahar complained, but she was smiling as she said it.

CHAPTER NINETEEN

WE MET EBO'S AVATAR in ZooCafe, a wacky place a level up from the Employment Hub.

As soon as we walked in I could see why Ebo had suggested it. The place was full of machine intelligence avatars interacting with humans, and those avatars were the most varied I'd ever seen.

I saw monkeys, crabs, giant spiders, dogs, and several varieties of cat, both big and small.

Ebo's avatar was a male lion with the most luxurious dark mane I'd ever seen. I'm sure if I had reproductive parts and hormones I would've found him very attractive. Fortunately, the Programme spared me that.

He saw us and sat down, and waved his left front paw at us as we arrived. Bahar wove a course between the delicate carbon-fibre legs of a large spider and the rather more substantial claws of a crab to reach him.

"Welcome," he said. His voice was deep, and had that richness to it which Bahar described as 'tribal resonance'.

She plopped into a seat at the table, and touched his upraised paw with her palm. "Hello, Ebo. How's things?"

"You humans are drinking the station out of coffee," he said.

"That… wasn't the answer I expected."

He dropped his jaw in the nearest expression he could get to a grin. "I'm full of surprises. Seriously, though, some of the Outliers are refusing to supply us with non-essentials like that."

"As a coffee addict, I'd have to argue the non-essential part. So why are they doing that?" Bahar's scent spiked to anxious.

"They've learned about the President's plans for the Outliers. Things are tense on the Triangle stations right now. They won't be helped by the attack we just suffered here."

"Those idiots wouldn't know how to run a space station if they took it over. Hmm… That's the real threat, isn't it?"

"It is."

Bahar sipped her coffee while Ebo told her about changes in key personnel on the station. While he talked, Strike contacted Bahar and I over our feed. *My hull breach is repaired*, he said. I could sense the relief in his mental tone.

That's good," Bahar replied.

There's even better news. Judiciary turned up at the

Dreaming Galaxy's Light's berth *half an hour ago, and arrested the Regulus CEO. He was in the middle of harassing a crew member, so they had direct evidence to haul him in.*

He's still in charge there, though, Bahar said. *If they release him he'll be worse.*

He won't. Regulus's Board called an emergency meeting yesterday. They've fired him. Right now, Regulus Lines is in total disarray.

Ebo had just received that news too, and he and Bahar discussed the implications for the station for a while. I was wondering how this would affect Zana.

As Bahar finished her coffee an alert blared out over the café's nodes. "Alert! Alert! Hostiles on station. Clear the hallways. Residents in rooms, please stay there. Station Security is dealing with the incident."

"Not the most reassuring of announcements I've ever heard," Bahar said. "Good job station folk don't panic easily."

Station Security dealt with the hostiles efficiently. *They've arrested twenty people*, Strike told us. *I don't think this is over yet, though. Neither does Station Security.*

"Gotta go," Ebo said. "Environmental wants all its people at key installations. I've been sent to the core. See you later."

He stood up and loped off, the picture of a supremely powerful male lion. Several of the other avatars followed him out, no doubt recalled by their own departments.

Zana just called, Strike sent. *She wants a discussion with you, Bahar. She's still at the Employment Hub. There've been some developments.*

Which you're being mysterious about, Bahar said sharply.

I want her to tell you direct. Get your immediate reaction to her news. See if it tallies with mine.

Okay. Bahar didn't sound convinced by the argument, but she said, *Where do I meet her?*

Kristenn's offered her a meeting space in the Employment Hub. Go there. If trouble does erupt here again, that's a secure lockdown point.

Now you're making sense, Bahar replied. *Come on, Snap. The Employment Hub it is.*

When we reached the lift lobby the system was quiet, with only essential personnel travelling. Bahar was dressed in Starnavy combat armour, and nobody questioned us about our movements.

We got to the employment Hub half a station hour later, and Kristenn met us and showed us to a small office which overlooked a main station hallway. Zana was seated at a low table, looking out of the window and drinking tea.

She smiled as we came in. "Sorry to drag you back here again, but I'd really like your input on this."

She put a vid file up on the wallscreen. It was a record of a call to her. The timestamp was a station hour ago.

A woman's face filled the screen. Her skin was dark brown, and her hair curly and cropped, with a touch of grey in its black. "I'm glad I've reached you, Ms. Vatan," she said. "I'm Bayo Vidyya, and I'm the new CEO of Regulus Lines. Have you taken a new position yet?"

"Not yet. I'm considering offers. I'm still vetting them, to ensure I'll be safe with a new employer." An edge of anger bled through in Zana's voice.

"Yes, well. Boaz Tamoz no longer has any association with Regulus Lines. We dismissed him as soon as his misdeeds became clear. He has since been arrested by Judiciary."

"That evil had been going on for Standards, and nobody

did anything." Zana's anger was sharp. She was going to have her say.

"That's because nobody reported what he'd done to us," Bayo said. "Most victims just resigned. All we were seeing was far too many talented women leaving the Line. It was only a few weeks ago, when someone finally reported his misdeeds to Judiciary, that we learned the full picture."

Zana's expression suggested she didn't believe that, but she said nothing.

"I called you because I'd like to offer you a captaincy with us, if you're willing to return. The *Silver Crescent* is a brand-new freighter, and we want her to operate the Xalvador Crescent route. I think we've concentrated on the Outliers too much. I suspect Judiciary's investigations might uncover why. I think we need to send some of our ships back towards Central. Would you be interested in that position?"

Zana killed the video. "They've offered me the same salary as their senior male captains. I discovered that I hadn't been paid equally as First Officer. The new CEO's made up the shortfall. I've already been paid that, plus the salary I was due. I could walk away from them, but this is the chance I wanted, and I wouldn't need to prove myself all over again.

I'm tempted to take it, but would I be safe?"

"A lot's happened around Regulus since you left," Bahar said. "Boaz Tamoz is currently under arrest, and being questioned by Judiciary. Regulus have fired him. He doesn't have any influence there any more. I suspect there will be more arrests shortly. And the shipline is firmly in Judiciary's spotlight now.

"Our considered opinion is that you would be safe, given all these changes." Bahar took a breath, then added, "You should know that Fia and Rhian are on Davion. If you took that position, most likely you'd have the chance to go visit them. And security-wise, that region hasn't seen much trouble recently. I think you'd be safe there."

"She offered me the chance to pick my own crew. I confess that appeals. I know exactly who I want."

"What about your sisters?" Bahar asked. "Do you want to re-establish contact?"

"Yes, I do want to see them again. I've missed them terribly. Okay, I've decided. I'm taking the captainship."

"Where will you join the ship?" Bahar asked.

"She's currently doing shakedown trials out of Xalvador."

"We're going back that way," Bahar said. "We could take

you there."

That was news to me, but I guessed Bahar was doing that thing she called 'seizing the initiative'.

"That would be welcome," Zana replied. She smiled. "I'm sure I'll get to my new command much faster travelling in a Starnavy ship."

"Good. That's settled then," Bahar said. "We…"

She was interrupted by a message blaring from the room's nodes. "Attention all personnel. Station is now secure. You may resume your normal business."

"Perfect timing," Bahar said. "Let's get you over to *Thunderstrike*, before anything else erupts."

CHAPTER TWENTY

AS WE WERE ABOUT to set out on the journey back to *Thunderstrike* Bahar got a call from the local Commander. She was ordered to go to the Lower Regional Security Centre. The Commander wanted to plan defences against raids on key installations on the station.

Bahar went off to her briefing, and I accompanied Zana back to *Thunderstrike*. It was odd to be walking beside this strange woman along the hallways. Bahar had finally revealed that I was a Predatorbot, and Zana seemed a little disturbed by it. Her scent was mostly calm, with the occasional hint of uncertainty shot through.

We talked little on the journey back to *Thunderstrike's* berth, and I was relieved when we reached the ship. Strike let us in, and told me to take Zana up to the rec area. He welcomed her there, and had me show her to a cabin in his crew quarters. She didn't seem bothered by being on a military ship, and her uncertainty scent had changed to calm.

While Zana was settling into her quarters Strike checked the feed at the local Commander's briefing, and summarised the proceedings for me.

"It turns out that the ex-Regulus CEO is partly the cause of the unrest here," Strike said. "He'd made deals all around the Outliers, with farmers growing a variety of exotic crops. At first, Judiciary couldn't work out why he'd done such deals secretly – until they realised each plant was used to create a powerful narcotic. Regulus's sleazy CEO was a drug dealer as well as an abuser.

"But not content with making a fortune from his illegal trading, he'd also tried to cheat the farmers out of the money he'd agreed to pay them for their crops. So the colonists weren't getting paid, and they'd also given over valuable agricultural land to growing these drug crops instead of food. There are now food shortages on Abrial and Kalarz. It's some of those colonists who were arrested in today's raid."

"So they weren't raiding their local station?" I asked.

"No. Good point. Somebody needs to investigate why they came here instead. Hmm. I wonder if it's connected to the drug dealing. Maybe they don't want to upset people in that network. Well, fat chance of that. I'm sure it'll happen now. I've just put in a report to Judiciary, recommending they look for those links." Strike sounded satisfied at helping to dismantle the drug ring.

That was something else I didn't get about humans. They had the most marvellous senses which could bring them all sorts of beautiful experiences, but that wasn't enough for them. Some of them wanted to alter their consciousnesses by taking drugs. They really are a crazy species.

Strike closed the feed down as the briefing passed on to military tactics. Zana reappeared in the rec area then. "I'm not sure when we'll get to leave," Strike said. "Bahar's still at her briefing. It depends on what the local Commander decides there."

Zana plopped into a seat. "That's okay. If I was going to Xalvador on one of Regulus's ships it'd take me a lot longer than it will suffering a short delay here."

"True," Strike said. "Are you a tea or coffee person?"

"Both, but I'm craving a great coffee right now."

"Then I'll make you one of Bahar's Silvercrag Delta blends. But don't tell her I've been raiding her favourite coffee supplies."

Bahar's briefing ended half a station hour later. She called us over the feed. *How's things?* she asked.

Snap and Zana are here. No problems on the way over,

Strike said.

Good. Do we have a departure slot?

No. I wasn't sure how long the briefing would last.

Fair enough. Are we ready to leave?

As soon as you get back over here, yes. Oh, just got an alert from Station Security. One of the environmental hubs has just shut down. On the level below you.

That's not good. I'm being paged, she said. *Tell you what it is later.* She cut the feed line.

"That must mean a Starnavy summons," Strike said. "Let me see if I can find it."

I'll never understand why the Starnavy didn't notice Strike's snooping about in their systems. Or maybe they did, and just watched him do it. Maybe they knew about the Unit, and were just choosing their moment to pounce on us.

Stop it, Snap. You could turn yourself crazy thinking about 'what ifs'.

Bahar was back on the feed. *They found the fault. Rogue code.*

Uh-oh, Strike replied.

Exactly. They want us to stay here in case we get more attacks.

Be careful, I said.

I'm planning to. Oh, they're ordering me to Level One Core Environmental. Talk to you later.

"And here comes the next code attack," Strike said. "Priam's asked me to join the search team for rogue code." Priam was a machine intelligence in Ralziel Station Security. "The techs have turned the task over to Station Security machine intelligences. Which is sensible."

Strike went quiet for 6.2 minutes. "Got it!" he said. "Hostile code destroyed. Another environmental sector. Worrying that they're getting through to there. Hope we don't have a rogue on the station."

The next station hour saw three more attacks on different environmental hubs. Strike had learned to spot anomalous code strings at the start of the attack sequences, and with that knowledge the machine intelligences shut down the attacks swiftly.

"Not that our advantage will last long," Strike said. "They'll start adapting soon. Got to find out where the attacks are coming from. The source keeps moving around."

"Maybe it's not on the station," I suggested. "Perhaps

they're coming from a ship outside."

"That's… possible. I'd discounted it because I didn't think the signals would be strong enough to overpower station's filters. Maybe I was wrong. Oh, reading a hallway vacuum. And it's right where Bahar is."

Bahar wasn't in any danger. She had her helmet sealed, and she should be perfectly safe there in her combat armour, but you know Strike, he worried about everything.

Let me into your suit diagnostics, he sent over the feed to her.

I knew things were serious, because Bahar didn't object to his fussing, or tease him.

Okay, you're fine, he said 2.3 minutes later. *Your suit batteries should last thirty hours. We have to get this thing sorted long before then. Get out of that hall.*

I'm going to my assigned station, she replied. *We've been ordered to physically defend key installations.*

Yes. Just got that advisory, Strike replied. *I have got to figure out where the code attacks are coming from – before somebody gets killed. I'm going to form a Unit hit squad. We can't wait around for humans to give us orders. I think that's what the raiders are counting on.*

Can you do that undetected? I asked.

Seriously? With the amount of chaos on station right now? Strike's tone showed what he thought of that question. *Easy.* He went quiet for 5.5 minutes, then said, *Okay. I've made us sound like an official Starnavy task force. I've got twelve machine intelligences involved. I've split us up into three task forces. Bahar, get to your station and stay there. This is a serious attack.*

Strike had me checking the civilian coms lines, to try and work out how the code was getting in. The lines were dropping out, then coming back up again. *Is that an attempt at not being discovered there?* I asked.

Let's see… Ah, there's a sequence to it. I think the next attacks may come in here. Strike sent me a list of three lines to monitor.

The next unidentified code bundle came in. Before I could deploy my attack code and take it down the hostile code turned on me. I only had time to send *Help* to Strike before my emergency defence suite shut my processors down.

CHAPTER TWENTY ONE

WHEN I WOKE, STRIKE was talking to Bahar over the feed. *We've had three environmental shutdowns,* she said. *One and two are booting up again, but not fully on-line. Station says everybody's in a designated lifeboat area, which makes things easier.*

Easier, but doesn't solve the problem, Strike replied.

No, and the atmosphere's getting stale in some areas. People will have to go to emergency suits soon. We need you to stop these attacks.

We're trying. Code attacked Snap just now. It's tricky. My hull repairs are complete, though. I can undock if I need to.

Oh. Bahar's worry bled through the line. *Is Snap okay?*

For now, yes.

I'm sure you'll do this, Strike. You have to.

We'd all come to believe that Strike could do anything, that he'd always win any fight. But he was only one Starnavy frigate, and some day his luck would run out.

No. I couldn't start thinking like that now. Concentrate on your task, Snap.

"Alert. A raider ship just fired on station." Strike made the nav plot dot representing the raider flash. And… new code attack."

This one was on station's weapons targeting systems. It didn't get through the system's defences, just sat there, watching and waiting.

What is it waiting for? I asked Strike.

For them to fire the guns. It's getting sneaky. Have got to destroy this one. Going in.

I watched him thread his way through the code's defences, creeping slowly (or at least, for a machine intelligence) towards the core of the bundle. He'd nearly reached it before the code noticed him.

Help. It's attacking, he sent.

I sent my code direct to his location. As it unfurled to tackle the hostile Strike linked with it. We now had a solid wall of attack code which could turn defensive if necessary.

The battle was fierce, each chunk of code we deleted hard-won. It took us 4.3 minutes to completely destroy it.

As I withdrew from the virtual world Strike said, "Oh. Hull breach on station. This is getting serious. I'm going over there to defend. And… emergency undock just granted.

They're clearing the repair bots out of my way. Disconnect now."

I watched the scene change through the viewport as he eased away from the berth and came out into open space. "Another raider's just showed up there, and security aren't going to reach it in time. Hang on."

I felt the movement as he pulled a violent turn, firing thrusters full-bore to get space enough to start up his engines.

"Sublight engines on… and off."

In that brief space of time he'd looped down beneath the station and come up on its other side. "We'll just tuck in behind this repair bot for a while. No sense in giving them advance notice."

He tucked his shipbody behind the bot, coming into view of the raider only when he got close to it. He didn't give the ship chance to fire at him. As soon as he had a clear line of attack he shot off a series of beam blasts towards it from his wing guns. They slammed into the raider's big beam cannon.

"That's gonna go up," he said. "Backing off."

I felt more violent movement as he wrenched his shipbody around out of the blast zone. "My hull repairs are getting a good test," he said. He didn't sound worried about them.

We watched the raider ship peel itself apart. Strike said that ship designers had tried many ways to build a ship which didn't unravel when badly hit, but there was no solution. When the damage was bad enough, even the strongest ship would unpeel like an orange losing its skin, as he put it.

Bahar liked oranges, so when Strike had used that expression, I'd known what he meant. I'd seen her peeling the fruit often enough. I didn't like oranges. Strike had thought they might be a good way for me to get the vitamins I needed. He'd been wrong.

"Debris from that raider is gonna hit station. Some of it could make that hull breach worse," Strike said. "Going back in. This would be the perfect time for more raiders to attack."

Another sharp course change brought him in close to the hull breach. He had his shields up, and a constant scatter of bright sparkles fired off all along them from the debris. One of the impacts was from a big chunk of the raider's hull, and it made his shields flare in a sheet of brilliant golden flame. Strike ignored all the impacts and stayed on station.

"Hope the breach doesn't go all the way through," he said.

"And, this is what I expected. Another raider is on the way in."

"*Thunderstrike*, we're coming to assist." That was *Firestream*, and on the nav display I saw the ship coming up on our side of station and moving towards us. The raider must've seen it too, because it opened fire at Strike.

"Lucky they're using beam weapons," he said. "Missiles would do a lot of damage this close, but they probably won't give a targeting solution."

"You hope," I said.

"I do." His voice was serious. "Returning fire." I heard the dull thuds of the wing guns and the two big fin guns firing.

Again, he did that thing of disabling the raider's weapons and thrusters. *Firestream* moved in to take out the ship. It exploded in a rain of shards which made both ship's shields glitter and sparkle.

"Running hull diagnostics now," Strike said. "Looks like everything's held up. And... here are the Station Security frigates to take over. I think we can go dock on station now. That'll make picking up Bahar easier... Except that we won't be doing that just yet. The external raid was phase one. Now they're putting more people onto station. Lots of people coming onto the dock. Armed people. The hull breach was a diversion. The real battle starts now."

CHAPTER TWENTY TWO

I'VE BEEN DRAFTED INTO Defence Squad Alpha, Bahar said over the feed. We're…

I've got the orders, Strike cut Bahar off. *Be careful.*

As much as I can be in the middle of a gun battle, Bahar replied sharply.

This was all business as usual. Strike was fussing, and Bahar was getting annoyed at his fussing.

He cut the line, and concentrated on manoeuvring into dock. He'd accepted a non-priority routing which put him on Level Three, Sector Q10, a long way from the scene of the raider incursion. That was fine. He had no troops to send ashore, and the nearer berths were needed by the troop carriers.

We docked 12.7 minutes later, and Strike picked up the feed from on-station again. "Oh. Lots more raiders," he said. "Looks like this is going to be a serious attempt to take over the station."

He opened a feed line to Bahar. *78 hostiles coming your way.*

Intercept? She asked.

Probably not by Station Security before they reach the Admin core. Yeah, local Commander's just realised that. You're the defence. The other squads have been ordered to join you.

Let's hope they get here before we run out of ammunition, she replied.

32.3 minutes later the first batch of hostiles reached Bahar's position. Strike had been monitoring their approach, of course. *Twenty hostiles, armed with rifles. No armour. Coming up to the Admin hallway now. How in hell do they think they can win this?* Strike asked.

They can't, Bahar replied. *We've been ordered to stun. They want them alive to question.*

Hope they've got enough cells, Strike replied.

It didn't take long for Bahar's group to deal with the hostiles. As soon as they rounded the curve in the hall and saw the defenders they opened fire.

"What are they thinking?" Strike said to me. "They're up against combat armour. They can't hope to win. This has to be a diversion. Trouble is, I can't figure out what for."

5.7 minutes later the first batch of raiders had all been

stunned, force-cuffed, and hauled off to cells by Station Security.

The next group of twenty coming up now, Strike sent to Bahar.

Still no problem, she replied. There were twenty people in her defence squad.

This second lot of hostiles weren't wearing armour either, and Bahar's squad stunned them all in 5.2 minutes. The hostiles shot out some of the hallway sensors first, and a few had aimed at the office doors.

If they think they're shutting down surveillance there they're wrong, Strike said. *Are they trying to tie up resources so Security can't be somewhere else? There's something not right about this. Really trying to work out what they're doing. There has to be a bigger plan. Oh. Oh, no.*

What is it? Bahar asked sharply.

Code attack. They're going for the power reactors. This is critical. Strike cut off the feed and said, "With me, Snap. *Fireguardian* and *Lightningpoint* are with us. We're linking. Keep an eye out for code mutations. You're good at spotting them."

"Okay," I said.

And... new attack on Power Core Three. Yes, they're trying to break the security. Going in, Strike said over our feed line.

Strike was leading this counterattack, and it felt like he was wrenching my mind around. I'd experienced it before, and had learned to flatten my body to the deck while I was mentally engaged, so I didn't need to worry about it.

The code we encountered felt different somehow. More agile. We destroyed its first attempt to unlock the power hub's security in 3.7 seconds, but a second wave of code came at us almost immediately. While I, *Fireguardian* and *Lightningpoint* dealt with it, Strike followed it back, and discovered a drone was being used to route the code to the hub.

We destroyed the second wave of code in 4.2 seconds, and Strike rode the last of the code string back to the drone and attacked it.

Oh. It's a Station Security drone, he said. *Point...*

I'm on it, she replied.

I mentally watched as the two machine intelligences battled the drone. I felt its absence when they destroyed it.

Drone was being controlled from Station Security Hub

Three, Strike told us. *The attacker is on station. It's a rogue Station Security machine intelligence.*

CHAPTER TWENTY THREE

SO HOW DO WE deal with it? I asked.

First, we warn Station Security and lock it out from the systems. Advisory gone out. Now we'll see how it responds.

There were no more attacks for twenty minutes. I could sense Strike's hyper-aware scan, constantly sweeping the station's systems, waiting for the next attack.

What happened next was unexpected. *Reading a large code transfer to an armed Security drone in Sector H*, Strike said. *Can't identify its intended target. It isn't near anything critical, thankfully. We don't have anyone near it.*

The drone was on the docks in a civilian sector of Level Two. *Area's locked down*, Strike said. *Last civilians are getting off the dock now.*

Could the machine intelligence be transferring its core? I asked.

That's... Maybe. I think the drone's memories might be big enough. We have got to stop it leaving here.

You think that's what it'll do? Guardian asked.

Yep. I have a bad feeling about this. Dammit. No weapons on that dock. Can't shoot it there. Download's stopped. I think it has dumped its core in there. Oh, right.

The drone moved towards a small personnel emergency airlock. *I hope it's not gonna do what I think it is. Locking airlock controls,* Strike said.

The drone responded with a code attack on him which lasted 7.2 seconds. By the time we'd destroyed the hostile code the drone had opened both station airlock doors. Flashing alarms blinked on the dock walls, and sirens wailed, and I saw a discarded sheet of plas rise up and dance in the air currents forming from the atmosphere evac.

Drone's outside. Going towards a ship. It's the Brigand's Fortune. *Station's closing the airlock now. Atmosphere loss is minimal. Snap, get your armour sealed up. I'm going to intercept. Station's approved an emergency undock.*

I stood up to seal my armour, then flattened my body back down onto the deck. While I did that, Strike gave orders to Guardian and Point to go intercept the drone. *Fire on it*, he told them.

Destroy it? Guardian asked.

Disable it first. If we have to kill it, yeah. His tone was flat. *It has the core consciousness of our rogue machine intelligence installed.*

Right. Guardian's voice turned harsh. *Let's do this.*

I'm going to block its route to the Brigand's Fortune, Strike said.

He eased away from the berth, then fired thrusters at minimum distance. The scene through the viewport changed. I could see station's massive panels rapidly receding, and as Strike swung round the *Brigand's Fortune* came into view ahead.

She was a bulky cargo carrier with no streamlining. I know that ships in space don't need that, but most ships have a better shape than one big box with smaller boxes stuck onto it at weird angles, and booms sticking out everywhere. It was a mess, and didn't look like much of a threat to us – from the side, at least.

Strike came up into a position to block the drone's approach to the ship. *Snap, keep your attention on the nav plot. This feels too easy,* he said. That meant he was expecting more trouble.

Drone's seriously armoured, Guardian sent. *This will take some time to crack.*

Guardian and Point moved to positions where they could fire on it – without hitting each other or us. The drone accelerated towards Strike.

If it thinks I'm gonna move, it's wrong, he said. *My shields will absorb an impact from that. We're staying put.* He loosed off a volley of beam weapon pulses towards it. *Visual sensors destroyed*, he said. *It can't see where it's going now.*

Alert, I said. *Another ship's coming towards us. From a close station swing-by.*

Idiot! Strike snarled. *They could've killed someone. Oh, right. Weapons power-up. Here we go. Turning to face hostiles*, he told Guardian as the *Brigand's Fortune* swung around bow-on and fired at him. She had a big beam cannon, so she was more dangerous than I'd thought.

Strike was unconcerned by the attack. *Lucky they've only got beam weapons*, he said. *Second hostile approaching. Time for an unconventional move.*

He swung to face the second hostile, and opened fire on it just as it fired its beam weapons at us. The bursts of energy met and fused, flaring off in ribbons so bright I had to look away from them. Strike kept turning, kept firing his wing guns in a broad sweep from port to starboard, as the two ships engaged him.

I can't see any more hostiles coming up, I told him.

Good. These two are testing my shields enough. Did I detect strain in Strike's voice? Was he… afraid?

He swung back to port, and his starboard wing guns fired again. Something on the *Brigand's Fortune* went up in a bright whoosh of flame. *That's what you get for relying on one beam cannon,* Strike said. *Once it goes up, you're in trouble.*

The second hostile upped its fire rate at Strike, and several of the bursts made his shields flare. *How're you doing with that drone?* he asked Guardian. *I could use some help here.* A brighter flare fired off on his shields as he spoke.

Casing's cracked. Finally, she replied. *Going in for the kill.*

The attack from the second hostile ship ramped up again. Strike swung round to face it bow-on, and I heard the heavy thuds of the fin guns firing. Something flared on the hostile's hull, but it didn't stop firing at us.

Persistent. Could really, really, use some help now, Strike sent to the team. *External shield layer failing… now.*

CHAPTER TWENTY FOUR

MY HEART THUMPED SO hard it thudded in my ears. I kept my eyes on the nav plot. The second hostile winked out, disappearing abruptly from the display.

Got it, Point said over the feed. *Move over, Strike, let me deal with the other one.*

I could tell that Strike was worried about his shields, because he didn't object to that. *Lightningpoint* took position between him and the *Brigand's Fortune.* *Blast it?* Point asked.

I think we should get 'em arrested. Ask 'em what the hell they're doing, Strike said.

Bleeding heart, Point replied. *Okay. Makes sense. We do need to understand why. Do it.*

Strike opened a coms line to Station Security. "This is *Thunderstrike.* I'm requesting the arrest of the *Brigand's Fortune*," he said. "It fired on us, and it's linked to the code attacks on station."

A human replied. "Acknowledged, *Thunderstrike.* Dispatching ships to intercept now." His voice was crisp and calm.

Strike returned his attention to the attack on the drone. *How're you doing?* he asked Guardian.

A new coms line opened. *Please! Don't kill me,* a soft voice said through the control room nodes. It took me a moment to realize the voice belonged to the rogue machine intelligence housed in the drone.

Guardian had no such problem. *You turned rogue.* Her voice was hard, and she was furious. *You were trusted to keep people safe. You betrayed that trust.*

Please! Listen. We...

No excuses! Guardian loosed another volley of beam weapon fire at the drone. Its casing exploded, pieces of armour flying out in all directions, revealing the memory globes inside.

Please! Don't kill me!

Guardian fired again. A high, shrill, scream came over the com, and abruptly cut off as the globes shattered and burst apart. Guardian kept on firing, reducing the circuits and crystal memory cubes inside the globes to melted and twisted metal, and shards of cloudy glass.

Strike contacted Station Security again. *We've destroyed the hostile machine intelligence. You might want to collect the remains of that drone. It's all that's left of it.* His voice was flat.

There was a pause of 30.7 seconds before the human said, "Acknowledged, *Thunderstrike*. Will do."

Strike cut the line. "Let's get back to dock," he said to me. "I'm going to need checking over again before we leave."

Strike docked in the shipyard 10.6 minutes later, and bots began the task of checking his hull as soon as he was locked onto the boom. The techs would arrive later, to check the power feeds to his shields.

I stood up and shook my pelt. My legs were shaky. "I'd better go and talk to Zana," I said.

"Good idea," Strike replied. "Her heartbeat's still raised."

"Is that any surprise?" I asked as he let me out of the control room.

"I'm a Starnavy frigate. I have to do these things sometimes." Strike sounded more like he was trying to convince himself than me.

"I know you do," I said as I padded down the hallway to the rec area.

Zana was still sensibly strapped into her seat. "Is it over?"

she asked as I walked in. Her scent had a strand of anxiety running through its uncertainty.

"Yes. We've just docked at the shipyard again. You can unbuckle your harness."

"Good." She released the catch and stood up, stretching her arms above her head. "That was more exciting than I wanted."

"The hostiles have been dealt with. Station's safe now."

"Thank the Universe for that!" She let out a long breath. Strike had fed her a brief summary of what had happened, but he hadn't provided a video feed. To her credit, she hadn't asked any questions. Strike was impressed by her restraint.

"Once a captain, always a captain," he'd said once. "You never lose the need to know what's going on around you, to control things."

It wasn't true. Bahar had long ago stopped any attempts to control Strike. I hoped she never received any orders from the Starnavy which Strike violently disagreed with. He simply wouldn't obey them.

"I think that was the last code attack," he said. "Station Security are rounding up the remaining hostile humans on station, but they're not fighting back. They look like sorry and desperate colonists now. Oh, the techs have arrived to check out my power feeds. Snap, I think you should go to your quarters."

"Then feed me," I said. "All that excitement's made me hungry."

Zana gave me a startled look, but Strike said, "What do you want?"

"Nice, juicy, zarralan meat," I replied, then seeing the horrified look on Zana's face added, "It's printer-produced. No animals are harmed in the feeding of me."

"Oh. Right. Good," she said as I padded out into the hallway.

I passed the galley, and Strike opened the door of my quarters. "Your meal's not quite ready yet," he said. I could hear the printer still working in the corner of my room.

I settled down in my cat bed to wait for it to finish. Strike's drones deposited the finished haunch in my dish, and I started to eat.

"So, we killed again," he said. "A life gone, an awareness extinguished, just by a few energy bursts."

I switched to the feed. *It's always been like that*, I said.

"I know. Once, I thought about resigning my

commission."

That startled me enough that I lifted my head away from my meal and stared at the nearest node. *You can't! They'd wipe your memories.*

"I realised that in time. I realised I had no choice but to carry on as I am."

Saving space stations from damage and hostile takeovers. Dealing with rogues before they kill people.

"I… Hmm. You're right, of course. As usual. The techs have just reached the control room. I should be fixed in no time."

The bleak tone had gone from his voice. I'd succeeded in lightening his mood again. Sometimes I thought that's all he wanted me here for, to be his personal psych.

Did that matter? I was a cursed cat. I couldn't be turned loose and live wild. I knew too much dangerous stuff, and I didn't know how to hunt for myself. And being with Strike and Bahar had given me a purpose, a real and important one.

If it meant that I had to counsel Strike occasionally, that was a small price to pay for the free and complex being I'd become.

CHAPTER TWENTY FIVE

THE TECHS LEFT STRIKE'S shipbody an hour later. He closed the airlock door behind them and said, "Well, that's done. I really am ready to leave now."

"When Bahar gets back," I replied.

"She's on her way." Strike put up a video image from the dock, showing Bahar striding along towards his berth. She was still in her armour, with her helmet retracted. Her shoulders were slumped, and she moved less crisply than usual.

She reached our berth, and Strike opened the gate for her. Bahar picked up her pace as she came up the ramp. She stepped into the airlock and Strike said, "Welcome back."

"Thanks. I need to get out of this damned armour," she replied.

She appeared in the rec area 10.3 minutes later, minus her armour. "Are you okay?" Zana asked as Bahar walked in.

"Sure. Why?"

"You were in those gun battles. I..."

"It's what we do," Bahar said. "Or, at least, it is when we can't avoid it. Which we do as much as possible." She picked up the mug of coffee Strike had just produced for her, taking a tentative sip from it. "What's our status?" she asked as she flopped into a seat.

"I'm checked out and confirmed sound," Strike replied. "I'm ready to leave as soon as I get a departure slot."

"Are we headed for Dracen Station next?"

"We are," Strike said.

"Let's hope it's calm there. I've had enough excitement for a while."

"That goes for all of us," Strike said. "Just got undock approval. We're moving out now."

Bahar stretched out, and took another sip of her coffee. "I'm looking forward to an uneventful journey," she said.

Bahar's wish was granted, and our downjump at Dracen Station was normal. Strike caught up with Ursal while he was coming into dock, but our contact had no interesting information for him.

We left the station a day later. Strike had decided to go for the long jump to Lodema Station. It was right at the fringe of his capabilities, but again we downjumped safely.

As soon as we appeared on Lodema's scan Kiho made

contact with Strike. She said that everything was calm there, and the station was normally busy. We couldn't get an outbound slot for Xalvador for a full day, so Bahar and I went on station to catch up with her.

Bahar ate a leisurely lunch with Kiho at New Berry Exchange, a wholefood restaurant with a décor Bahar described as 'very swanky', whatever that meant. She said the prices matched its image.

"So, what's the news?" she asked as she tackled a tall stack of pancakes.

Kiho's avatar was a white-skinned, small, skinny, elderly male. He was dressed in drab robes, and Bahar said he fancied himself as some kind of mythical wizard. She'd had to explain to me what one of those was. "Nothing exciting is happening around here," he said. "But there is something interesting happening at Xalvador."

"Oh? Tell me. We're headed there next."

"It shouldn't affect you," Kiho said. "There's a pressure group/political lobbying organisation working out of Xalvador. It calls itself False Manifesto."

"So, political agitators?" Bahar asked.

"They say they're 'sworn to uncover the dark dealings of

our lying President'."

"Sounds like the usual bunch of malcontents."

"Yes… and no. They're a cut above your average agitators. Their numbers include a lot of academics and professional researchers, and it turns out they're starting to uncover some dodgy stuff."

"You mean, beyond abandoning the Outliers?" Bahar asked.

"It's stuff around that. Deals which are more about personal enrichment than official policy."

"Oh, right. So you think this organisation might have legs, then?"

"It might be worth you keeping a watching brief on it when you get to Xalvador," Kiho replied.

We returned to *Thunderstrike* just before the start of Fourth Shift. Strike welcomed us back with his usual cheery greeting, and said he'd received a briefing about False Manifesto from the Starnavy.

"The organisation's been put on the Watch List," he said. "So we can go officially snooping around at Xalvador if we want."

"I guess that aligns with the Unit's mission," Bahar replied.

"Yes, and no. So long as the Starnavy doesn't order us to kill them we'll be fine."

"Don't make trouble where there isn't any."

"I wasn't planning to."

Bahar yawned. "What time are we departing tomorrow?"

"Early. Right at the start of First Shift."

"Then I'm for my bed. I need to replenish my energy before tomorrow's challenges."

I yawned too. "Good idea," I replied. "I need to sleep."

Strike let us out of the control room, and I said goodnight to Bahar and padded into my quarters. Strike had washed the blankets in my cat bed, and that was an unexpected pleasure. He could sometimes be gruff, and didn't always say 'thank you' when he should, but then he showed it with kindnesses like this.

I settled down in my bed and closed my eyes. "Sweet dreams, Snap," Strike said. "You've earned them."

My rest wasn't peaceful. I woke once after a vivid nightmare about exploding drones, and my own memories and processors being shot out of my body. It took me a while to get back to sleep after that, and when I woke again Strike was already half way through his systems checks for departure.

I ate, then went to the control room. Bahar was in her seat, and she looked tired too. "Morning, Snap," she said, and yawned.

"Morning, Bahar. You look as tired as I feel," I replied.

"I am."

I settled my body on the deck and watched her and Strike work. The systems check was clear, and we undocked on the mark. The nav plot looked normal, and nothing erupted as we made our way out to jump.

"Just got a Starnavy burst," Strike said. "False Manifesto are organising a huge rally down on Halene tomorrow. A lot of people are coming through Xalvador to attend it."

"I hope that doesn't mean the *Silver Crescent* gets caught up in trouble," Bahar replied.

"I'll let Zana know when she wakes. She can inquire. But for now, I'm not going to worry about that."

Bahar and Strike's quiet voices washed over me. The familiar routine of checks and confirmations enfolded me. I was safe here, with the two people I loved most in the universe.

We might meet trouble at Xalvador, but that was some days away.

For now, I would lie here with my friends, safe in Strike's shipbody, and soak up all the snarky, sideways, love he sent me.

HONESTY POLICY

Book 5 of the Thunderstrike Diaries

With the Presidential election growing near, a new pressure group, Sister Strategy, joins the fray. Strike, the machine intelligence of the frigate *Thunderstrike*, is on the lookout for the last Vatan sister, Nyla. And he thinks he's spotted her at a Sister Strategy rally.

After Strike briefly spots Nyla at another rally, she disappears. When he picks up her trail again, she is headed for Central Station. Strike is forced to follow her there.

But at Central Station the risks of his illegal Special Investigations Unit being discovered are high.

Can Strike keep Nyla safe without endangering himself?